Zomcats!

Zomcats!

Book II of the Jack D McLean zombie series

Jack D. McLean

For Martin Mulligan
A true friend

Part I: England

Chapter 1

Henderson the cat had no business stalking a muntjac deer many times his own size and weight; the fight was sure to be uneven, and the odds very much favoured the deer.

He dropped into a crouch, slunk forward through the undergrowth, and pounced. The muntjac made a plaintive bark as it lost a chunk of flesh from its flank. It made its second and final bark as Henderson ripped out its throat, and died instantly from shock. The cat feasted on its corpse then pushed on over the bleak Yorkshire moors, looking for bigger and better prey.

Just over the next hill, directly in his path, lay the Yorkshire village of Nobblethwaite.

Chapter 2

A stone whistled past Bob Slawit's ear, missing it by millimetres and almost knocking him off balance.

"Ha, ha ha! Nice one, Nipper!" Said Bigfucka Briggs.

Bigfuckaa was the leader of the Savages, a teenage gang that had been terrorising the villagers of Nobblethwaite for months.

Encouraged by the words of his leader, Nipper Davies pranced up behind Slawit and gave him an energetic kick up the backside. Slawit turned on his attacker, waving his white stick angrily. Unfortunately, he was unable to see much more than a dark shadow which danced nimbly out of range as he swung his stick at it.

"I'll 'ave yer, yer little bastard," he fumed impotently, as more stones came his way. "I'll make yer bloody well pay."

As the word 'pay' left his lips, a particularly large stone hit him on the forehead. He staggered backward from the force of it, blood spurting onto the cobbles from the wound it had made. He dropped his stick and covered the wound with his veined old hands.

"Yer little bastards," he cried, as another kick up the backside sent him sprawling onto the cobbles.

"I'll have yer, I'll have the lot of yer," he said, waving his fists in the air, as boot after teenage boot landed sickeningly in his ribs.

Slawit had spent most of the afternoon sinking pints of real ale in the Ne'er Do Well, the only pub in the village.

After that, he'd gone to the Nobblethwaite McDonald's and enjoyed a Mega-Bucket of extra-thick blackcurrant milkshake which had bits of something gritty alleged to be real pieces of blackcurrant floating about in it. As the boots struck home, Slawit felt the milkshake and the eight pints of real ale he'd drunk sloshing about his insides in a sinister way.

A boot caught him in the pit of his stomach.

He rolled onto his back and opened his mouth to say "Oh Fuck," but no words came out.

Instead, a dark purple fountain spurted from his mouth at high pressure. In size and ferocity it resembled a volcanic eruption. It shot into the air, forcefully covering his attackers in vomit. It coated them all liberally, and they fled in disgust, covered in foul-smelling goo.

Once they'd gone, Marjory, the kindly old lady who ran the village bakery, came out of her shop and helped Bob to his feet.

"They're right little terrors, that lot Bob," she said.

"That's not the word I'd use to describe them," he replied. "I'd describe them as right little twats."

"Well, I don't blame you. I just hope they 'aven't hurt you."

"You what? You hope they haven't hurt me? Did you see what they did? Course they hurt me, the little twats."

"I'm sorry. I would have helped but I'm scared to death of 'em. I didn't want to risk getting beat up me self, and nor did anyone else round here. We're all scared to death of 'em."

"What about that copper we have that's meant to be on the village beat? Constable Bryson. Why didn't he come to help me?"

"There's been a lot of coppers made redundant from up at the Nab Police Station, Bob. So, Constable Bryson has to cover ten villages now. He only comes to Nobblethwaite every second Monday and on Bank Holidays."

"I'll go and ask that gang of young twats to wait till a week on Monday or the next May Day Bank Holiday to beat me up next time then, eh? That way Copper Bryson might have some chance of seeing 'em at it and arresting someone."

Marjory picked up Slawit's stick and handed it to him.

"I'm very sorry Bob, truly I am."

"Sorry if I was a bit short with yer. I was angry that's all. It's a good job I were shit-faced cos if I hadn't been I would have felt every one of those bloody kicks. I'll see thee Marjory."

"Bye bye Bob. Take care, now."

"I will."

Slawit made his uncertain way to the side of the road and tapped around with his white stick to get his bearings, then he tapped his way up Nodger Hill, the steep incline which led to Slawit Hall, his home, which was perched alone on the top of the hill, a mile outside Nobblethwaite.

When he got there, he heard a meowing noise as he opened his front door.

"Who are you, little pussycat?" He asked. He bent down and let the unseen cat rub its face against his hand, then he stroked the cat under its chin and touched a collar and name tag. He ran his fingers over the name tag, reading the engraved lettering with his fingertips.

"Henderson," he said. "So that's your name. Where have you come from? You better come in."

He pushed open the door as the cat rubbed against his legs.

"Now then," he said. "I expect you'll want something to eat."

"Meeow. Meeow. Meeeeoooow."

"I'm not hungry me self, but I'll get you something."

He opened a kitchen cupboard packed with canned food and groped around with his hand.

"I think you'll like this, lad," he said, grabbing one of the cans. "I'm pretty sure it's got meat in it."

He opened the can, scraped the contents onto a side plate, and put the plate on the floor.

The cat sniffed it and walked away.

"Meeow," he said again.

"What?" Slawit asked. "You couldn't have eaten it that quickly. That's not possible."

He reached to the floor and felt around and soon enough his fingers encountered a pile of stewed steak in gravy.

"You fussy little bugger," he said. "Well, if you're not 'aving that, I am. I'll save it for me self to eat later."

He put the plate in his fridge and searched with his fingers for the leftover bacon on the top shelf.

"You can have this instead."

He threw the bacon to the floor. Henderson snarled as he pounced on it. He held the meat down with his abnormally large paws, while tearing bits from it with his sharp teeth.

"I've never heard a cat make noises like you do. Yer sound more like a lion than any cat I've ever met," said Slawit, when he heard Henderson's voracious eating.

"Meeow, meeow, meeeeooow."

"You can't still be hungry. There must 'ave been at least three quarters of a pound of bacon there. Hang on, I'll see what else I can get yer."

Slawit groped in his fridge, and found four beef sausages. He lobbed them to the floor and heard a snarling, chewing sound followed by the cat purring. Then:

"Meeow, meeow, meeeeooow."

"For God's sake, I can't keep up with yer. I haven't got any more food left in the house. You'll have to wait till tomorrow to be fed, when I next go to the shops."

Slawit went to his front room and tried to read one of his brail books, but it was impossible because of the noise.

"Meeow, meeow, meeeeooow."

"Hell's teeth," he said. "I've had enough."

He went to the front door and opened it.

"Go on," he said. "Out yer go."

"Meeow, meeow, meeeeoooow."

As Henderson was showing no inclination to leave, Slawit went to where he thought the cat's meowing was coming from, and prodded around with his white stick. He didn't mean to hurt Henderson, merely to shift him out of the house.

Henderson began playing with the end of the stick, and grabbed it in his mouth. When Slawit found he couldn't move the stick any more, he tried to push Henderson away with his boot. Henderson let go of the stick and playfully sank his teeth into Slawit's boot then pulled them out again.

"Fucking 'ell fire," said Slawit, quickly retracting his foot.

Blood was spraying from the holes the cat's teeth had made. Slawit hobbled around in a panic, while Henderson eagerly licked up the blood that was dribbling over the kitchen floor.

"Got to get outa here," Slawit muttered.

He tapped his way upstairs to his bedroom and shut the door.

Then he heard a noise on the landing:

"Meeeow meeow."

He hopped around in a panic until he'd located his chest of drawers and shifted it as best he could against the door, then hopped to his bed and collapsed on it, breathing heavily.

Meanwhile, Henderson padded downstairs. He knew that kindly humans who fed him at night would generally feed him in the morning too, so he returned to the kitchen and found a cardboard box to curl up in. Then he waited patiently for Slawit's return. After a while he nodded off and dreamed of a terrible accident he'd had some months previously.

He'd been run over by a car which had squashed his midsection flat and killed him.

The next thing he knew, he was waking up in the cellar of his next-door neighbour, Professor Ted Forsyth, who lived at 41 Acacia Avenue in the London borough of Sutton, near Croydon.

Forsyth had built a machine he called the 'Lazarus Engine', and he had used it to raise Henderson from the dead. Unfortunately, the process hadn't quite worked as planned, for it hadn't truly brought Henderson back to life; instead, it had turned him into a zombie cat, or zomcat. Moreover, it hadn't done anything to fix his midsection, which remained flat as a pancake and resembled the blade of a circular saw, owing to his vertebrae protruding up from it.

While Henderson lay in the kitchen dreaming, Slawit got his breath back. As soon as he felt he could move again, he reached out to his bedside cabinet where he kept his telephone, picked up the receiver, and dialled 999.

A young male voice answered his call.

"This is the Emergency Services. Which service do you require?"

"The bloody ambulance service, and be quick about it, and the police, and probably the fire engines too."

"I'm sorry, sir, what is the emergency? Is it a fire?"

"No, it's a cat. At least that's what I thought it was, and I let it into me house. But I think I've got the Beast of Bodmin Moor in me kitchen or something just like it, and it's tried to take me bloody foot off. I need help fast. I daren't leave me bedroom. I swear to God it'll 'ave me if I do."

There was a long pause followed by:

"All right, putting you through now, sir."

A deeper and more mature male voice took over.

"West Yorkshire Police here. Have you been drinking, sir?"

"What's that got to do with anything? I'm in fear of me life. Send some help around right away."

"What appears to be the problem, sir?"

"A wild animal I let in me house. I thought it was a cat but it's not. It's a bloody panther or something like that."

"When you let it in, couldn't you see what exactly it was, sir?"

"No I bloody well couldn't. I'm blind."

"All right, I'll send a car round. What's your address?"

"Slawit Hall, Nodger Hill, Nobblethwaite. And I need an ambulance as well."

"Very good. What's your name, please?"

"Slawit. Bob Slawit."

"On its way for you, Mr. Slawit."

Slawit collapsed on his bed.

After what seemed an interminable wait, there was a knock on his front door. He recognised it immediately as a policeman's knock. He'd heard one before, many years ago, when, as a child, he'd broken a neighbour's window and the police had been called to investigate. After the police had been and gone, his father had given him a leathering of the sort that the twats could have done with on a daily basis.

He heard his front door opening, then he heard the voices of the policemen.

"Christ almighty, what a smell. Doesn't he ever clean this place?"

"Maybe he does, but it must be hard for him, Ben. He's blind."

"Oh God, that pong. It's enough to make yer eyes water. Hey, Charlie, hang on a minute. What was that?"

"What was what?"

"I just saw something move in the kitchen."

"Didn't that bloke Slawit say something about a cat?"

"What I just saw was no bloody cat. Get your truncheon out, Charlie. That's it. Oh my God, have you bloody well seen it?"

"I've never seen anything like it. If it gets anywhere near either of us, give it a good whack. Where's my pepper spray?"

Slawit heard a sound like an angry cat hissing, and another sound like a policeman's truncheon hitting something fleshy but very solid. Then he heard:

"Aaaargh!"

"Aaaaaaarrgh!"

He listened for the reassuring sound of coppers' feet coming up the stairs to his bedroom, but none came, not even after ten more minutes. There was just an eerie silence, so he called the emergency services again.

"It's Bob Slawit here, of Slawit Hall," he said, when he was finally put through to the police. "You've just sent a couple of coppers around to me house to see off this animal that's been terrorising me. Yer need to send reinforcements fast."

"Why?" The young man who'd taken his call asked.

"I think the two you've just sent me are dead"

"What makes you think that, Mr. Slawit?"

"They came into me house twenty minutes since. I didn't see them, because I'm stuck up here in me bedroom. Anyway, after they came in, they both screamed. Blood-curdling screams they were, and since then I've heard nothing from them. Not a dicky bird. So, I reckon they must've happened some'at. Some'at that didn't do them a right lot of good, if yer get me drift."

"All right, Mr. Slawit, I'll try to contact the officers now, and see what they're doing."

"Yer might as well contact the bloody undertakers while yer at it, for all the good that'll do."

"I'm sure there's no cause for alarm, Mr. Slawit. Please be patient. I'll have to end this call now, so that I can deal with your problem. Your number has come up on my system. I'll call you back if we need to talk further. Good bye."

"Get yer best team of SWAT men up he-"

12

The line went dead.

"Fucking arse-holes, honestly!" Said Slawit.

He lay down on his bed listening for cat noises, but all he could hear was the rapid beating of his own heart.

Chapter 3

The man at the Nab police station who'd spoken to Slawit got on the police radio. He heard it ring out to Ben and Charlie, the two constables who'd been sent to Slawit's house, but there was no reply. He radioed Jenny Blackshaw and Keith Foster, two constables who were in a patrol car near Nobblethwaite.

"Jenny, Keith, there's been a report of two of our men going down at Slawit Hall."

"What's happened to them, Brian?"

"They're said to have been killed by an animal of some kind. It's probably nothing, but I can't get in touch with them. The householder's a local character called Bob Slawit. He's got a reputation for being a bit of a nutter. He says he's trapped in his bedroom. I think he's been drinking. Anyway, I need you to investigate right away."

"Ten four" said Foster, who liked to imagine that he was a member of the California Highway Patrol, and not just a British Beat Bobby in a crap car.

Jenny put her foot on the accelerator and they sped, blues and twos, to Slawit Hall.

They pulled up in the street outside, and climbed out of their car. It was dark, and the lone house reared up against the night sky. There were no lights on in the house so they switched on their police torches as they approached the front door, which was open.

They went inside with truncheons drawn, just in case, tried the light switches, and found they didn't work. They entered the front room and saw nothing amiss.

They walked into the kitchen and directed their torch beams around the walls then onto the floor.

"Oh. My. God." Said Foster.

There, in front of him, were the bodies of his colleagues Ben and Charlie. Both had been badly mauled, and Charlie looked as if he'd been half-eaten.

Blackshaw looked at her feet and realised she was standing in blood. For a moment she hesitated, unsure of whether to leave the crime scene for fear of contaminating it, or to approach her colleagues to check if either of them was alive, although that seemed impossible. Nevertheless, she decided that she ought to check, and quickly went over to them. A cursory glance by torchlight when she was up close told her all she needed to know.

She looked at Foster and shook her head.

"Whatever did this, it might still be around," said Foster. "Better keep your wits about you. You call for backup, and I'll keep watch."

He took out his pepper spray and held it in one hand with his torch in the other, while Blackshaw called headquarters.

"Okay," he said, when she had finished the call. "Let's see if we can find the householder."

They crept upstairs in the darkness with only their torches for illumination. When they reached the landing, Blackshaw called out.

"Mr. Slawit. Mr. Slawit! It's the police."

"Where have you lot fucking been? I've been stuck up here scared shitless for the last two hours."

She tried the bedroom door, but it wouldn't move because the chest of drawers was shoved up against it. Foster put his shoulder to the door, they both pushed, and it inched open.

They shone their torches into the bedroom. Slawit was on his bed, the bottom end of which was dark red with dried blood. There was a trickle of blood coming from one of his boots.

"I'll call an ambulance," said Blackshaw.

"Haven't you got one?" Slawit asked. "I bloody well told 'em to send one."

The ambulance took two hours to arrive. When it did, Slawit was stretchered inside and taken to the Accident and Casualty department of the Nab Hospital, where he was given a tetanus injection, patched up, and discharged.

By noon the following day he was holding court in his favourite haunt - the Ne'er Do Well pub.

"I tell yer, it wore the Beast of Bodmin Moor," he said to a walker who'd spent the morning hiking over the moors, and gone to the pub for a refreshing pint, little knowing that he'd be buttonholed by the village bore as soon as he entered the place.

The locals all knew to keep their distance from Slawit. Even the fact that he was partially sighted wasn't enough to earn him the pity to be listened to, these days. They'd all had enough.

"But Bodmin Moor's over three hundred miles south of here," said the walker.

"Well, it couldn't have been anything else. Unless it wore a cougar," said Bob.

The walker was half-minded to say "don't be ridiculous," then he relented.

He saw Bob's white stick and noticed that Bob's eyes never seemed to be quite looking in the direction they should, and he knew that Bob had serious eyesight problems. He felt sorry for him.

He wished he could ask "How would you know? You're blind?" But he couldn't. You didn't treat blind people that way. And besides, he told himself, the old man with the broad Yorkshire accent was probably a half-wit. He certainly sounded like one.

"A cougar, eh?" He said. "I bet you don't get many of those round here."

The walker tried hard not to sound sarcastic when he said it, but some small note of doubt about the veracity of Bob's story must have entered his voice, because Bob said:

"Are you being a clever bugger, or what?"

"No," said the walker, "Not at all. I was just saying, you don't get many of those around here. Cougars, I mean. Nor beasts from Bodmin Moor, I expect." He used the most sincere tone of voice of which he was capable, and this seemed to placate his partially-sighted drinking companion.

"Yer don't," said Bob. "And I hope to God it stays that way. It's killed two men already. They were a right bloody mess."

"What were?" The walker asked.

"The two men. The ones that got killed by the animal in me house."

"When was that?" The walker asked politely.

By now he was convinced that Bob Slawit was unhinged.

"Last night. I shudder to think what'd happen if we had more than one of them things on the loose running around the village. We'd all end up as cat food."

"Quite" said the walker. "That would be beyond the pale, wouldn't it?"

"Yeah, I'm Bob by the way," said Slawit, holding out his hand expectantly.

The walker saw how grubby it was, and quickly slipped on a glove before shaking Bob's hand. He made a mental note to wash the glove as soon as he got the chance.

"I'm Owen," he said. "Owen Blackhead."

"You should see me foot," said Bob, raising it from beneath the table so that Owen could get a good look at it. It was covered in bandages. "If I've got one stitch in me foot, I must 'ave got five hundred."

"That looks painful," said Owen, planning his escape.

He downed what remained of his pint in one gulp and stood up.

"I really must be going now."

"I'll be going me self soon. I need to go and get me self some nosebag."

"Cheerio – er - what did you say your name was?"

"Bob Slawit."

"Cheerio, Bob. I'll see you when I'm next in Nobblethwaite."

But not if I can help it, he thought.

Slawit raised his head, his oddly pale eyes darting around randomly.

"Goodbye, young man," he said, and Owen felt for a moment quite flattered, being well into late middle age.

He left the pub and went to the village bakery for further refreshments, where he was served by Marjory. He felt he could indulge himself with a clear conscience, having just walked the better part of twenty miles over difficult terrain.

"I'll have a slice of apple pie," he said. "In fact, make that two slices, please."

He handed over his money, and Marjory handed over his order.

I'll make short work of those, thought Owen.

Before he could grab the bag containing his goodies, he was interrupted by a commotion outside. It was the sound of shouting and laughter. But this was no ordinary shouting and laughing; it sounded evil.

Chapter 4

Owen looked out of the shop window to see what was causing the noise. He saw a gang of five youths standing in a circle. In the middle of the circle stood the partially-sighted bore he'd been talking to in the Ne'er Do Well: Bob Slawit. Owen couldn't hear what was being said, but it was obviously not friendly.

Slawit looked panic-stricken. The youths hadn't done anything to him other than shout at him, but that was enough to have shaken him up. And no wonder, thought Owen. I'd be shaken up if I had that lot around me, shouting and laughing. He might not be able to see them, but just from the sound of their voices, he'll know what they're like.

Owen took the paper bag containing his apple pie from Marjory. He felt he ought to intervene and stop the youths from taunting the old man. At the same time, he worried about what might happen if he did.

Owen Blackhead was a big man, standing over six feet tall, but it was a long time since he'd been involved in any trouble of a physical kind. He was in his forties, and the last time he'd been in a brawl was in his teens. He'd been slim, strong, and quick, when he was a teenager, and he hadn't enjoyed the experience of fighting even then; now, as a middle-aged man, carrying, as he admitted himself, some timber he could do without, he knew that he was ill-equipped for this sort of thing. Still, he couldn't let it go on without at least trying to help in some way.

He decided to remonstrate with the youths, and set his face determinedly. Then he turned towards the door, his heart pumping a little faster at the prospect of the confrontation that lay ahead.

"I wouldn't go out there if I was you."

It was Marjory, the shopkeeper.

Owen stopped, grateful for the excuse to delay his mission.

"Why not?" He asked.

"That lot are the Savages, one of the gangs from the council estate up the road. If you try to help Bob Slawit, and I can see that's what yer minded to do, they'll 'ave yer. They'll get you on the floor and they'll kick lumps out of you. You'll be leaving the village of Nobblethwaite in an ambulance."

Owen froze to the spot, his heart beating even faster. He looked out of the window again. The boys were prodding Slawit now, as well as laughing at him. The old man was cursing and making futile gestures with his white stick. One of the youths darted up to him and slapped him in the face, so hard that it spun Slawit's head to one side. Owen saw a trickle of blood leave the old man's mouth.

That's it, he thought, I've got to do something. I can't let this go on.

He left the bakery and marched with the most confident gait he could muster up to the gang of youths. As he approached them, he realised that even though they were all probably only in their mid-teens, four of them were the same size he was, and one of them was considerably bigger than him.

Owen's stomach dropped to his knees, which became oddly weak. He forced himself through the fear barrier and carried on going until he was within a few feet of them. Close enough to make his presence felt, but out of arm's reach so that none of them could sucker punch him.

He wondered whether he should threaten them or be diplomatic. He decided to try diplomacy.

If I do that, he thought, I might get away without any argy-bargy.

"Lads," he said. No-one took any notice.

"Hey, you! You lot! That's right, you! I'm talking to you!" He shouted. They all turned towards him.

Five pairs of eyes were directed at him, none of them friendly.

Owen wondered if he'd done the right thing. But there was no going back now.

Behind the gang of unfriendly youths, he was vaguely aware of Bob Slawit leaning on his white stick and shaking.

"It's not fair, five of you picking on an old man," said Owen, adopting a tone of voice that he hoped would sound like the voice of reason.

"We could pick on someone younger, couldn't we, lads?" Said Bigfucka, grinning.

"Why don't you find something better to do with your time?" Owen asked, wondering how he could climb out of the deep pit he felt he'd fallen into.

The gang forgot about the old man and advanced on Owen.

"There must be something more constructive for you to do," Owen ventured, a note of desperation entering his voice.

"Aye, there is," said Bigfucka. "But we prefer demolition to construction, don't we lads?"

His crude joke provoked evil guffaws amongst his companions. Owen knew now that whatever he said, he'd have a fight on his hands. It was such a long time since he'd been in a fight, he didn't know what to do. He mixed in middle class circles now, not like he used to when he'd been growing up in Barnsley, and his new values hadn't equipped him to deal with this sort of circumstance. His current lifestyle was all about being reasonable and debating your differences with other people, not flattening them if you disagreed with them.

He tried to remember how he'd handled situations like this in his teens. Not well, he remembered, not even then, when he'd been at the height of his physical powers, but at least he'd been able to run away, and lash out if he was cornered. He had bad knees these days, so running away was out of the question. As for lashing out, he lacked the reflexes he'd had in his youth.

He struck up a fighting pose with his fists raised, hoping against hope he wouldn't have to use them.

"See that, lads?" Said Bigfucka, all thoughts of Bob Slawit having gone from his mind for the time being. "He thinks he's a boxer. This is going to be fun."

Oh fuck, thought Owen. I should have stayed in the shop.

Bigfucka came towards him with the others close behind.

This was it.

Owen drew back his right fist, hoping he could at least land one blow, preferably a haymaker, before they got him on the ground and kicked him half to death.

Then he heard a strange noise, a noise which changed everything.

Chapter 5

It was a deep growl, like that of a lion, or tiger.

Owen and the Savages turned their heads in amazement to look at the source of the noise.

It was Bob Slawit.

His face was twisted and angry, but not in the way a human being gets angry. His features had taken on a feral quality. He growled again, and this time it was more threatening than before.

Bigfucka laughed.

"What does he think he's playing at?" He asked. "Does he think he can scare us by growling at us?"

Slawit dropped his stick and held up his arms with the elbows bent and his fingers curled as if they were claws.

"He's gone fucking bonkers!" Said Nipper Davies.

"I always knew he was bonkers," said Bigfucka.

Slawit opened his mouth, stuck his head forward, hissing loudly.

That was when they saw his teeth. He'd developed long canines, like a big cat, and the rest of his teeth had become pointed. He dropped on all fours and hissed again, his face twisted even more, if that was possible.

"I'm not having this," said Bigfucka. "If he thinks he can scare us by putting a set of joke teeth in his mouth and hissing like a tabby cat, he's got another thing coming."

Bigfucka took a short run up, and, after drawing back his right leg, booted Slawit full in the mouth. But Slawit, even though he was blind, sensed the kick coming, opened his jaws to receive Bigfucka's foot, then closed his teeth on it. He clamped them down, and blood sprayed in all directions from Bigfucka's foot.

"Aaaaargh!" He cried. "He's a bloody nutter. 'Elp me."

He tried desperately to extricate his foot from Slawit's mouth, but Slawit held on to it.

Nipper Davies picked up Slawit's white stick and began beating on his back, but it didn't seem to hurt Slawit, who closed his jaws tighter, severing Bigfucka's foot in two. He turned his head to one side, chowing down on the half-foot he held in his mouth, including the half boot that had come with it.

Bigfucka's blood surged like a fast-flowing river from the remains of his boot. He fell to the ground crying, while nursing his leg in his arms.

Owen backed away, baffled by the strange turn of events. He'd felt out of his depth before, but this wasn't a matter of mere depth, it was a matter of something else – something alien. The situation was totally outside his experience. Bigfucka had got no more than he deserved, Owen thought, and now it was he who needed Owen's help. But, Owen wondered, was he willing to stay around and give his help with that thing on the loose, whatever it was?

Nipper and the rest of the gang tried to get Bigfucka to his feet.

Slawit finished the food he had in his mouth. He'd suddenly acquired a covering of ginger fur, and his eyes no longer darted randomly around. His pupils narrowed and turned red. He sniffed at the river of blood on the pavement, then raised his head to see where the blood was coming from. Bigfucka was on his feet by now, with his arms across the shoulders of two of his cohorts, one to either side of him. Nipper Davies got between them and Slawit, waving the white stick in Slawit's direction, in an attempt to keep him at bay. The other two gang members were cowering behind Bigfucka.

Claws emerged from the ends of Slawit's fingers. He shrunk, and became more muscular. His ears moved up towards the top of his head and grew points on them.

He wriggled free of his clothes, and pawed at the white stick as if it was a plaything. Nipper Davies made the mistake of prodding him in the face with it. That was when he pounced.

Within seconds, Davies was on his back.

"Gerrofferme!" He shouted, as Slawit tore his face off.

"Let's get outa here lads!" said Bigfucka.

Owen considered this to be sound advice, and fled to what he thought was a safe distance. He watched the rest of the goings on from the corner at the end of the road. He took out his mobile and tried to film the incident, but his hands were shaking so much that he didn't get any clear images.

Nipper stopped protesting, then stopped moving, and Slawit lost interest in him. He looked up to see Bigfucka trying to make his getaway.

Perhaps there was some vestige of human memory left in Slawit, allowing him to remember the torments that Bigfucka had put him through; or possibly he was driven simply by bloodlust. Whatever the reason, he pounced on Bigfucka, pulling him to the ground.

Bigfucka's last pleading words were: "I'm sorry, Bob, honest. I was only playing, I didn't mean to hurt you, or anything. Please let me go, will you? Please?"

The words were still leaving his mouth when Slawit ripped off his lips.

The last thing he said wasn't a word, indeed, it fell short of being even a syllable.

"Wwwwwwww…"

When Slawit had finished with Bigfucka's face it looked like it'd gone through the electric mincing machine in the butcher's shop on the village High Street. It was a new model, the BVR 600 De Luxe, which could mince an entire cow in under two minutes. The way Bob Slawit was shaping up, he was almost a match for it.

Having minced up most of Bigfucka, he went after the remaining three members of the gang, and did for them all in short order. By the time he was done, the high street was awash with blood. The villagers, who'd all stayed indoors because of the threat of the gang, locked and bolted their doors when it became evident that Bob Slawit, or the thing that Slawit had become, was a bigger threat than the gang had ever been.

Marjory called the police.

"Send someone out here quick," she said. "It's a cat, or a man-cat, and it's killing people."

"I'm sorry, what's happening, madam?"

There's something out there and it's attacking people."

"Very good, madam, what's the address?"

"The village high street, Nobblethwaite."

"A car is on its way Madam. Please tell me again the nature of the emergency."

"There's a big cat and it's attacking folk. Send an ambulance and men with guns."

"How big is the cat?"

"About the size of the ginger tom that lives next door but one, Frederick he's called. He's a right little bugger, he keeps shitting on my geraniums."

"So, about the size of a domestic cat?"

"Yes, but a very big domestic cat."

"And it's attacking people. What's it doing to them?"

"So far it's ripped some throats out, minced a man's face, and torn another man's lips off."

"And a cat has done all this, you say?"

"That's right, a bloody cat."

"Thank you, madam. I'll pass the information on to the team who will be sent to assist."

During the two-hour wait for the emergency services to arrive, Slawit stripped Bigfucka's corpse bare of flesh, and then he set off exploring. An instinct took him in the direction of Nodger Hill. He came to the street corner that Owen Blackhead was hiding behind – more cowering than hiding, if truth be known – and stopped for a moment when he saw Owen.

Owen looked at the cat and felt himself shrinking with fear. He would have tried to run despite his bad knees, but his legs felt incapable of carrying his weight.

The ginger cat that Slawit had become stared at him with an unflinching gaze and then, for reasons which can only be guessed at, ignored Owen and continued its journey up Nodger Hill.

Owen was so relieved that he collapsed to the ground. When he'd recovered his wits, he got to his feet and went back to the Ne'er Do Well pub.

"I'll have a triple whiskey please," He said to the landlady.

The man next to him had also ordered a triple whiskey. He turned to Owen.

"Did you see that? I've never seen the like. What the hell was it?" He asked.

Owen shook his head.

"I dunno. I still can't believe what I saw. It could have been a were-cat if there is such a thing."

"I don't know what the hell it was either, but I'm staying in here till the police arrive."

Chapter 6

A police car pulled up outside the Ne'er Do Well and two uniformed constables climbed out, Keith Foster and Jenny Blackshaw. The streets were deserted. They walked along the high street until they came to the body of Nipper Davies. He was lying face up, or at least, what was left of his face was directed at the sky, with unseeing pits for eyes. Nearby there were four other bodies, all equally mutilated.

"Oh my God," said foster. "It's like last night, only worse, much worse."

He walked around the perimeter of the death zone, trying to work out what manner of man or beast could be responsible for such carnage. He didn't bother to check whether any of the victims were still alive. It was obvious they couldn't be, especially Bigfucka Briggs, who was far and away the deadest of the lot of them.

"Jenny, you better make sure you've got a weapon in your hand. Whatever did this might still be on the loose."

"I'm way ahead of you, Keith," she said. "The report said it was a domestic cat that did this. Some cat."

"It couldn't have been just an ordinary domestic cat. I bet yer some rich nutter got a panther or something like that as a pet, and then let it go when it grew up and got to be too much of a handful. That's what a lot of these rich nutters do. I'll radio for back-up, and I'll ask for forensics as well."

"We ought to get in the car till the back-up gets here. We're not equipped to take out a big cat."

"You're right."

An hour later the back-up arrived, equipped with tracker dogs, rifles and tranquiliser darts, and led by an Inspector.

"Let me remind you of the procedure," he said when they got out of their cars. "Keep everyone indoors until we've made sure the thing isn't in the village. Remember, it's a killer, so we're not risking tranquiliser darts, we're using live ammunition. Have you got that?"

"Yes, sir."

"Make sure you stay together in your teams of two while you're on patrol, and look out for each other. Don't take any risks. No-one is to go anywhere on his own."

"Got that, sir."

The CSI began his examination of the crime scene, while the tracker team fanned out, checking the few roads and gardens in the small village, and established that the threat was no longer present.

The Inspector told his team to advise all the villagers that Nobblethwaite was free from the threat of big cat attacks for the time being, but they should stay indoors as much as possible until the animal was known to have been eliminated, and should only venture outdoors when absolutely necessary.

Then, witnesses were found and interviewed.

It soon became evident that only two of the witnesses had seen the whole episode from beginning to end, Marjory Jones, the proprietor of the Village Bakery, and Owen Blackhead, the walker.

Jenny Blackshaw interviewed them both.

"Let's get this straight, Marjory," she said. "I'll go over it one last time. You saw Bob Slawit being terrorised by a group of youths who call themselves the Savages. He turned into a cat – a bigger-than-average cat, but not a big cat like a tiger - and he killed them all."

"That's right," said Marjory. "I know what I saw, Constable."

Marjory was beginning to wonder if she did know what she saw. Even when she'd been watching it happen, she hadn't quite believed it.

"Is it possible you saw a cat savage the Savages and in all the confusion, you just imagined that the cat was Bob Slawit?"

"No. Er, yes. Er, well, I don't know, I'm sorry."

"All right, never mind Marjory."

Her interview with Owen in the Ne'er Do Well was similarly confusing.

"It was a cat, you say?"

"Yes, constable, and if there is such a thing as a were-cat, it was a were-cat."

"What's a were-cat?"

"A werewolf is a man who turns into a wolf, otherwise known as a lycanthrope. This was a man who turned into a cat. So, you'd call him a were-cat, or a felinethrope. I've got a video of it."

Owen held up his mobile and showed Blackshaw what he'd recorded. There was so much camera shake going on that it was impossible to make anything of the images he'd captured.

"Where's the footage of the man changing into a cat?" Blackshaw asked.

"I didn't start filming till after that had happened."

"Thank you, Mr. Blackhead, that'll be all for now. I'll be in touch if I need to interview you about your evidence again."

Blackshaw stood up and left the pub, shaking her head as soon as she was out of the door.

She noticed the tracker teams all heading in the same direction. Their dogs seemed to agree that whatever they were after had gone up Nodger Hill.

Chapter 7

There were four teams, with four dogs between them. The dogs lowered their snouts to the pavement periodically, then moved forwards in pursuit of their quarry.

Their handlers followed close behind, each accompanied by a marksman with his rifle at the ready. The dogs neared the top of the hill, then stopped, and began whining and squealing. They refused to go further.

"I've never seen them do anything like this before," said one of the handlers.

"It could mean we're almost on it," said another.

The marksmen raised their rifles. The dogs retreated to the back of the group of men, and cowered, quietly whimpering.

Ahead of them was Slawit Hall, large and threatening, with the bleak Yorkshire Moorlands behind it. A wind blew, and the front door creaked open.

"I bet it's in there," said one of the men. "I bet it's bloody well in that house."

Chapter 8

"What're we gonna do about it, if it is?"

"We can't risk going in. Let's surround the place and smoke it out. When it shows its face, we'll blow its bloody head off."

The teams fanned out, leaving their dogs tethered to the gateposts at the end of the drive leading up to Slawit Hall. As they moved forwards, a ginger cat which was slightly bigger than a domestic cat emerged from the front door, heading calmly in the direction of the moorland. One of the men raised his rifle and drew a bead on it. Then he said:

"No, that can't be it. That's just a bloody cat. No point in blowing that to bits, it'd be a waste of ammo. Might as well save it for the real thing."

Once the place had been surrounded, the team hurled smoke bombs through the windows. They waited and waited, but nothing emerged. They tried using their tracker dogs again, but the dogs either failed to find a scent, or were reticent to follow it.

As dusk fell, the Inspector gathered the team together.

"All right, we best call it off for now," he said. "We'll go home and have a meeting tomorrow first thing to plan our next move."

Chapter 9

It was the year 1743.

Lord George Slawit, who owned the village of Nobblethwaite and all the land around it as far as the eye could see, was standing in front of Slawit Hall, his ancestral home. He was about to mount his horse when an old gypsy woman appeared at the end of the drive. She walked towards him. He narrowed his eyes, looked at her, then got on his horse and galloped over to her.

"This is private property," he said. "What do you want?"

"If it pleases your Lordship," she replied, "I 'ave some wooden clothes pegs for sale."

She raised a basketful of pegs she was carrying so that Slawit could see them properly.

"What would I want with a load of stupid pegs?" He demanded. "Get off my land before I horsewhip thee, thou ignorant old crone."

"I will get off thine land, Lord Slawit," she replied. "But afore I do, I'm going to put a curse on thee. And forevermore, folk round here will talk of the curse of the Slawits that laid your family low."

She began chanting and waving one of her arms around, still clutching her basket with the other. Slawit raised his hand with his horsewhip in it as if to strike her, and she turned and fled.

"Good riddance!" he shouted at her fast-disappearing back.

One of his gardeners had heard the exchange and he looked up from his weeding with a troubled expression on his face.

"What art thou looking at?" Slawit demanded. "Get back to thine work thou nosey bastard before I raise my hand to you."

The gardener quickly turned away.

From then on, the fortunes of the Slawits went slowly into decline.

Chapter 10

It was the year 2016.

The Ne'er Do Well was packed with villagers getting trolleyed. The landlady had a wood fire burning in the grate, and everyone was talking about the events of the day.

"It was Bob Slawit, I tell yer. He turned into a cat. I saw it with me own eyes."

"Don't be such a daft bugger, Sam. I saw it too, but I never saw Bob Slawit doing 'owt. It was a cat, a bloody big cat, like a tiger, only ginger."

"It wore never a tiger. It wore more like a lynx."

"Bugger you and your lynx. It were a bobcat."

"What's a bobca-"

At that moment the door opened, and a stranger entered the pub. He was young and carrying a rucksack. He walked confidently to the bar. Heads turned to look at him.

"Good evening," he said to the landlady. "I'd like a pint of the Magic Rock Pale Ale please."

She pulled him his pint and he handed over a ten pound note.

"Can I ask you for some directions?" He asked.

"Of course," she said "fire away."

"I'm looking for Slawit hall, the ancestral home of my family."

Everybody stopped talking. The room fell silent, and the young man felt eyes staring at him.

"What's wrong?" He asked. "Have I said something I shouldn't?"

An old man with a twisted lip sidled up to him.

"We don't like talk of Slawit Hall round 'ere lad," he said. "It's nothing personal. It's just that there's a curse on t'place."

All around the pub heads nodded, and people could be heard muttering "That's right," and "It's t' curse of t' Slaw-its".

The landlady gave the young man his change.

"Don't take any notice of them," she said. "They don't know what they're talking about."

"Oh aye," said a man sitting at a table near the bar, "how do you explain what happened this afternoon, then? You know - Bob Slawit turning into a were-cat and killing five young men in t' street outside?"

"Bob Slawit is my grandfather," said the young man. "I'm James, the last in the Slawit line. Are you saying something's happened to him?"

"We are that lad, he's turned into a bloody tiger or something like that, and he's going round tearing folk to pieces."

The landlady shook her head.

"No-one can prove that," she said. "There's only a couple of people claim they saw him do that. One of them is Marjory, She's nice enough, but she's not the sharpest tool in the box is she? And t'other one who says Bob Slawit turned into a were-cat was that young walker, but he's not from these parts. I bet he's not playing with a full deck, either."

The old man looked away and muttered to himself, and the villagers got back to their drinking and general murmuring.

The landlady leaned across the bar and spoke to James in hushed tones.

"There's a big hill at the end of the high street called Nodger Hill, with a cobbled road running up it. You'll see the sign for it just outside. Follow the cobbled road up to the top. That's where you'll find Slawit Hall. Be careful, mind, we've had five killings in this village today, and there's some as reckon a big cat did it, and some as reckon it might 'ave been some other animal, and even some, as you know, as reckon your grandfather turned into a cat and did it. So, watch your step. If you'll take my advice, you'll stay here in one of my rooms for the night, and go there tomorrow during the day."

The young man finished his pint.

"That's very good of you," he said. "But I don't believe in all that superstitious nonsense, and I've been waiting a long time to be reunited with my grandfather. I'm not waiting any longer."

"It's not superstition that five men were killed in t' Nobblethwaite high street today."

"Maybe not, but my mind's made up. If it was an animal that did that, it's probably long gone by now. And anyway, I've got this."

He took a number of objects from of his rucksack and started putting them together.

"What've yer got there?"

"It's my shotgun. I thought I'd get some shooting done on Grandfather's estate while I was up here. This thing will stop anything that moves."

"Aye, but will it stop a were-cat?"

"We'll just have to see, won't we?"

James Slawit put his rucksack on his back and left the Ne'er Do Well with his shotgun nestled in the crook of his arm. He saw the sign for Nodger Hill and walked towards it up the high street. He came to the line of police tape around the area where the gang known as the Savages had been slaughtered. At that point, he thought he better have his shotgun ready for action, so he loaded it with a couple of 12-bore cartridges, and made his way up the steep cobbled incline of Nodger Hill.

Shortly after James left the pub, Sam Bateson finished his pint.

"That's it," he said. "I've had enough. I'm going home."

He wiped the froth from his white whiskers, got to his feet, and wobbled backwards and forwards until he'd found his equilibrium.

"Mind how you go out there," said the landlady. "There mightn't be anything supernatural like a were-cat on the high street, but there's some 'at that'll 'ave yer if yer get in its way."

"Don't worry," said Sam. "I'll check if the coast is clear then I'll go straight home. I only live across the road."

He opened the door, looking right and left. The street was dark, and all was quiet.

"It's all right, everyone," he said. "There's nowt to be scared of. There's nowt there."

No sooner had the words left his lips than he heard two shotgun blasts, followed by what the villagers would later describe as a blood-curdling scream.

Bateson immediately retreated into the safety of the pub, slamming the door shut behind him.

"Did you hear that?" He asked, his eyes open wide.

"Aye, I did," said Bog Jessop. "I reckon as we all did."

There were murmurs of agreement from all around the pub.

"What are we going to do?" Bateson asked.

"I'm 'aving another pint," said Jessop.

"Me too," said someone else.

"I reckon as I'll join you then," said Bateson.

It fell on the landlady to call the police, which she did as soon as she'd pulled all the pints of beer that were suddenly required by everyone.

Chapter 11

Up at the Nab police headquarters, they were all in a tizzy.

They'd had seven dead bodies within seven days, and the landlady of the Ne'er Do Well in Nobblethwaite had just called in with news that suggested there might be an eighth. The trouble was, no-one at the Nab had any great desire to go out to Nobblethwaite late at night and risk another life, investigating yet another death. But they had no choice. What were they to do?

Commander Bradshaw clutched the straws together in his clenched fist.

"All right, lads," he said. "You know the rules by now. Here you go."

He extended his hand, and a number of young police constables and older sergeants assembled in a semi-circle front of him. They stepped forward one at a time, drawing straws from his hand.

The tension mounted as every straw that was drawn proved to be a long straw. Finally, there were only two straws left.

Keith Foster stepped forward and took one. He held it up for everyone to see. It was the short one.

"Oh, hell," he said. "I knew I should have gone for t'other bugger."

His colleagues gathered around him, giving him supportive pats on the shoulder.

"Hard lines Keith," one of them said. "Better luck next time, if there is a next time, of course."

"That means it's not just you that's fucked, Jenny Bradshaw's fucked too, isn't she Keith?" Another said. "She is your partner, isn't she? Where is Jenny tonight?"

"She's getting a brew," Said Keith. "I'll let her enjoy it before I tell her the good news."

Keith found Jenny and explained the situation to her, then they signed the documents which allowed them to carry firearms while on duty, took their rifles from the police arsenal, and went to their car.

They drove through dark country roads to Slawit Hall, where they could confirm that there had indeed been another death caused by something capable of ripping a man to pieces. They reported the incident to headquarters.

They were about to leave when Jenny heard a low growl.

It was the last thing she ever heard.

Keith got lucky. He got to hear his own screams before he died.

Chapter 12

After leaving Nobblethwaite, Owen Blackhead returned to his home town of Huddersfield.

He had a blog called 'The Hiking Dad', which was devoted to his experiences as a walker. As soon as he found the time, he put a lengthy post in it about the were-cat he'd seen in Nobblethwaite. The post had a very positive impact on visitors to his blog. The numbers leaped from three a month to over three thousand an hour. As an added bonus, most of the visitors passed comment on his post, something which had seldom happened before, certainly not in those sorts of numbers.

Owen was delighted.

Until he read the comments.

That was when he decided he had to get proof that were-cats existed.

Chapter 13

It was a hole, and not just any hole, it was a fucking massive hole.

But what made this different from other holes was that it was full of shit.

Farmer Hodge was looking at it contemplatively while holding his nose.

Perhaps it's time to dig a new hole, he thought. The Hodge family has been using this one for generations, but now at last it's full.

The thought never once occurred to Farmer Hodge to get a septic tank installed at his farm. He was a Yorkshireman, and he was far too careful with his money to ever squander it on a frivolity like that.

He scouted around the field looking for a suitable spot to dig a new hole, and when he found the ideal location for it, he got his tractor rigged up with his excavator tool, and dug the biggest hole he could. Then he climbed down from his tractor, and stared at his new hole with a look of satisfaction on his face.

Next I'll have to re-route some of the soil pipes from the previous hole to this one, he thought. I wonder how long I've got before the old hole overflows.

He looked up to see a man in the distance dressed in hiking gear ambling along Stonker Lane. That bastard better not be thinking of walking across my land, he said to himself. He wandered over to the first of his family's shit-holes and examined it carefully.

There was a slight breeze which was causing the surface of the shit to ripple, like the waves on a lake. Where they lapped against the edge of the hole, they were almost, but not quite, flooding the dry land surrounding it.

It's probably good enough for another couple of hundred shits, he said to himself. By then it'll be brim-full, so I better not leave it too long to re-route those soil pipes.

Then he had a pleasing thought:

Maybe I could run a footpath from the road right up to this shit-hole, he said to himself. Then when those annoying bastard walkers walk over my land in future, some of them might fall into that old shit-hole of mine. Hopefully one or two of them might even drown in it.

There was no danger of any hikers using the proper footpaths on Farmer Hodge's land; he'd made sure they couldn't use them. He'd blocked off the gap in the wall at the side of the road which gave access to the legal footpaths on his land, and he'd run barbed-wire fences across them for good measure.

When he'd finished smiling to himself at the thought of the new footpath, Farmer Hodge parked up his tractor next to his farmhouse and went inside for a cup of tea. While he was drinking his tea in the kitchen, he resolved to build the new footpath leading to the shit-hole the very next day.

After a good night's sleep, Hodge rose at 4.00 a.m., showered, dressed, and set to work on the new path. He ran it in a straight line from the old shit-hole to the wall that separated his land from Stonker Lane, and he created a new opening in the wall which positively beckoned walkers to enter through it onto his new path.

The lie of the land was such that the shit-hole couldn't be seen until you were almost on it, and in calm conditions, when the wind wasn't rippling its surface, the shit-hole looked like a huge area of bare earth in the middle of a field which for some unaccountable reason had a profoundly bad smell hanging in the air above it.

Those ignorant bastard walkers won't be able to tell its shit, thought Hodge with satisfaction when he'd finished work on the path. They'll think it's bare earth and assume this is what a farm smells like.

Hodge had perhaps underestimated the intensity of the smell that came from his shit-hole.

He slept well that night, and got up in the morning feeling positive because it was the tenth anniversary of his divorce from his long-suffering ex-wife. He'd been so pleased to see the back of her that he had a little celebration all by himself on this date. They'd never had children; he was the last in the Hodge line. It didn't bother him, as he hated children.

He put on his green wellington boots and ventured out into the farmyard.

Chapter 14

After killing Charlie and Ben, the two unfortunate policemen who'd gone to rescue Bob Slawit, Henderson left Slawit Hall by the open front door and set off through the night. He instinctively headed back towards Huddersfield, perhaps because it had been his last real home.

At dawn he found a sheltered spot beneath an overhanging rock. He curled up under it and fell asleep, dreaming of his old owner in Croydon, the kindly Mrs Thompson. She'd taken him in when he'd been a stray, and looked after him until he'd been killed in a car accident then turned into a zombie cat by Professor Ted Forsyth.

At length he woke up, yawned, and stretched. It was time to start walking across the bleak and wild terrain of Nobble Moor again.

As dawn broke on the fifth day of his journey, Henderson found himself crossing the outlying fields of Stonker Edge Farm. He made his way across them to a patch of long grass near the farmhouse, and there he stopped.

Directly ahead he could see Farmer Hodge emerging from his front door wearing his green wellies.

Henderson couldn't understand why, but he associated Hodge with bad things happening to him. This may have been because Hodge had discharged his shotgun close to Henderson's ear, some months previously, or because some instinct told him that Hodge was a cat-hater.

He dropped into a low crouch, as low, that is, as he could manage with his disc-shaped midsection. Then he wiggled his backside. When he was certain that Hodge hadn't seen him, he walked stealthily a few paces closer to his prey and stopped again.

Hodge, unaware of the danger he was in, walked in Henderson's direction. The zomcat wiggled his backside one last time and set himself. Hodge started whistling a tune, as he cheerfully contemplated the many walkers who were going to come to grief in his shit-hole.

He got no further than the first few bars of his cheery tune when something came at him from the long grass a few yards ahead, something resembling a ginger thunderbolt. It flew into the air and hit him in the face. For an instant he felt as if he was being savaged by a bramble bush, and fought hard to escape its painful clutches. But the ginger brambles were sharp and dug into his flesh, and the branches of the ginger bush had a ferocious strength to them. He felt its teeth sinking into his neck.

The farmer whirled his arms in a panic, crying out as his blood sprayed in all directions. He saw it – heard it – splashing on the side of his ancient Ferguson tractor. But he didn't see it for long. First his left eye came out, and a nice juicy morsel that was, and the right eye soon followed it.

Mad with pain and blind, Hodge ran across his farmyard shrieking with Henderson still clinging to his head.

Mr. and Mrs. Beadles were walking along Stonker Lane, having come all the way from Farnley Tyas in Huddersfield to do a spot of bird watching. They heard Hodge's screams.

"What were that?" Mr Beadles asked.

"Ah don't rightly know," his wife replied.

Mr. Beadles had a pair of binoculars slung around his neck. He raised them to his eyes.

"It's just some daft bugger larking about," he said. "Here, have a look at him."

He passed the binoculars to his wife.

"Ah see what yer mean," she said. "The dozy sod's wearing a ginger Davy Crockett hat. It takes all sorts, ah suppose."

She lowered the binoculars and the two of them continued their walk along Stonker Lane.

After a while, Mr. Beadles said:

"Ah think Ah'll just take another look at what yonder daft bugger's up to."

He raised the binoculars to his eyes again.

"Y'know Margaret, I'm not sure it's a Davy Crocket hat he's wearing after all. In fact, I'm not even sure it's a hat. It looks like something's attacking him, some sort of a wild animal."

"Let me 'ave a look."

She took the binoculars.

"Y'know, I think yer right. We better go 'elp the poor bastard."

There was a dry-stone wall preventing them from cutting straight across the fields to the farmyard where Hodge was having his life forcibly taken away from him. Neither of them fancied the thought of scrambling over the wall. Mr Beadles pointed.

"Look Margaret, there's an opening in t'wall further along. We can get through that."

The two of them hurried along Stonker Lane to the gap in the wall, and went through it onto the path at the other side. It led in a straight line towards the farmhouse.

"We better hurry," said Mr. Beadles, breaking into a run. Mrs. Beadles did her best to keep up with him.

"Christ," she shouted as she ran. "It stinks around here."

"All farms do!" Her husband shouted back.

The stink got worse as they neared the farm. Directly ahead of them, the grass gave way to what looked like a very large patch of bare earth. Mr and Mrs Beadles ran straight onto it. Or rather, into it. For a brief period their cries for help competed with those of Hodge.

They desperately tried to swim for the shore, but there was no getting out of the mess they'd gotten into. It was too deep, too viscous, and far too sticky.

Mr. Beadle's last thoughts as he disappeared below the surface of the shit were: "Oh fucking hell."

Hodge, meanwhile, had lost so much blood that he could no longer scream. He couldn't even stand up. He dropped to the ground, and felt his lips being ripped from his face. It was only the first of many such torments he was obliged to endure that day.

After eating his fill of Farmer Hodge, Henderson felt sated. He decided to stay at Stonker Edge Farm for a while because the food there was plentiful. The fields were full of it, walking around and mooing all day long. He found a barn with some hay in it he could lie on, and then he dozed off. As dusk fell, he woke up, strolled to Stonker Edge, and contemplated the town of Huddersfield which was spread out in the bottom of the valley, far below.

It was to be his kingdom now.

He decided to romp down there, have sex until dawn, and possibly a picnic or two, then return to the farm to get himself fed again and have another kip.

Chapter 15

It was deathly quiet in Bert Fossett's back garden, but he wasn't fooled. He knew that sooner or later, the cat that had been shitting in his vegetable-patch every night for the last week would put in an appearance. This time, he'd be ready for it. He was a keen gardener, and he wasn't going to have his seasonal autumn crops of carrots, leeks and marrows ruined by a cat. So he sat on his back doorstep keeping watch with an airgun in his right hand.

The lights in his house were out, and there were no streetlights anywhere nearby, so Fossett's back garden was illuminated by little more than the night sky. It was a cloudy night, which meant that his garden was a very dark place. But that didn't worry Fossett. He'd bought a pair of night-vision goggles to ensure he'd be able to see the intruder when it arrived.

He was wearing his outdoor jacket and woolly pullover, but even so he began to shiver. He'd been outside for several hours, and felt as if the cold night air had begun to penetrate the many layers of clothing he was wearing. He put down his airgun and blew on his hands, then picked up his airgun again and rested his hands on his knees. He was getting increasingly uncomfortable, and he could have done with going indoors and warming himself in front of the fire, but he wasn't going to be beaten. He was determined to see his mission through to the bitter end, and he was convinced that the end would indeed be bitter, at least for the cat that he'd become obsessed with. For him, however, it would be sweet, for there was nothing in his world that was sweeter than revenge.

He heard a subtle rustling sound from the privet hedge bordering his garden. He looked in the direction the sound had come from and saw a cat's head poking through the bottom of the hedge. He watched as it eased itself through, holding its belly close to the ground.

Wait for it, he thought. Let it get all the way in so that I've got a good big target to aim at.

Slowly, silently, he raised the gun and drew a bead on the cat. It seemed to get itself stuck under the privet for a moment, and then it made an extra effort and popped through into his garden. When it did he lowered his gun and looked more closely at it. The animal was like no other cat he'd ever seen. It was half again as big as the other cats around Birkby that occasionally made the mistake of pestering him, and it had an odd distinguishing feature: The middle of the cat between its forelegs and hind legs was flat, like a pancake. The top of its arched back had a series of sharp-looking spikes on it, like the blade of a circular saw.

What the? Fossett thought.

The cat raised its tail and sprayed a jet of fluid over Fossett's privet to mark out its territory. Fossett smelt it, his blood pressure rising. He raised his airgun again, but his hands were shaking with anger and when he pulled the trigger he shot wide of his target, sending the pellet whizzing harmlessly into the privet. The cat turned its head to see what had caused the noise. When it had established there was no threat, it strolled languidly into the middle of Fossett's vegetable-patch and dug a small hole. Fossett re-loaded his airgun and pointed it, just as the cat nonchalantly began to drop a very large log into the hole.

This time his hands were shaking so much that he sent the pellet through one of the windows of his own greenhouse.

He rose to his feet in a state of fury.

"Fuckin' bastard cat," he said.

The cat was by this time making a cursory attempt to cover up the mess it had made in the middle of Fossett's crop of baby marrows.

Fossett strode purposefully over to it, imagining he was playing for Huddersfield Town, the football club he supported through thick and thin, mainly thin. He pictured himself in front of an open goal with the ball at his feet, and gave the cat the hardest kick he'd ever given anything in his life. He caught it with the toe-end of his boot right under its deformed belly, hoisted it off the ground, and sent it flying through the side of his greenhouse. There was a jangling noise as the cat sailed through a pane of glass, followed by a crashing noise as it fell amongst a pile of ceramic plant pots.

"Good riddance to bad rubbish," said Fossett. "I'll 'ave to replace those broken panes in me green arse but it'll 'ave been well worth it."

The cat landed on its feet and shook itself, sending the splinters of glass that had been embedded in its fur flying in all directions. It then charged straight through the glazed wall of Fosset's greenhouse, sending many more splinters of glass flying. When it was through, it stopped, and stood looking at him for a couple of seconds, then lowered itself so that its belly was close to the ground, and wiggled its buttocks.

Fossett had watched cats often, and he knew much about their habits and behaviour, so he knew what that meant: the cat was going to charge, and pounce on its prey. And he realised that he himself was the prey.

"Why, you cheeky little bastard," he said.

He spread out his arms with his hands palm-up, paddling his fingers up and down as if intending to start a bar-room brawl.

"Come on," he said. "Fucking bring it on."

The cat charged at him. Fossett was ready with his boot but the cat jumped up high, and landed on his head, rendering his poised boot useless.

He staggered back, his head a mass of pain and torn flesh.

A neighbour's bedroom window opened.

Fossett was vaguely aware of it, and he tried to call out for help.

"Hel-aaargh!" He cried.

"Oy, you, keep the noise down. It's four in the morning and I've got to get up for work tomorrow! And you can take that silly bloody hat off your head."

Fossett heard the window being slammed shut as he fell to the ground in a state of blinding agony.

"Fucking bastard cat," he said.

They were the last words he ever spoke.

The cat dragged his corpse under a large bush and feasted on his head along with much of his torso.

Chapter 16

Tiddles lived in Birkby, the outlying area of Huddersfield at the base of Stonker Edge. She'd gone out for the night against her owner's better judgement, and followed her nose, which led her inevitably to a large lump of freshly killed meat: the corpse of the late Bert Fossett.

She sniffed around it for a while, wondering whether to eat some of it, or go in search of field mice, when she was pounced on by Henderson.

He sank his teeth into the scruff of her neck and mated with her. As Henderson was still full of Fossett, he didn't bother to eat Tiddles. When he'd done with her, he moved on and found another three female cats called Sally, Becky and Florence. They were given the same treatment.

All of them were infected with the zombie virus he carried.

Chapter 17

He left his home in the small hours and swaggered down the garden path, looking neither left nor right. He walked down the street as if he owned it, and in a sense, he did. He was the cock of the walk in those parts. That was because he was very big for a domestic cat. In fact, he was so exceptionally big his size had led to him being featured in a story in the Huddersfield Examiner. The week the newspaper ran the story, it had been so stuck for an interesting news item (a frequent occurrence with the Examiner) that it ran the following breathless headline on the front page: 'World's biggest cat lives in Hudds!' The rest of the page was taken up by a photograph of Goliath next to his owner's young daughter, whom he dwarfed.

Goliath was fat and lazy and unafraid. He was a black monster who terrorised all the other male cats in the neighbourhood, so when he encountered Henderson, he fluffed up his fur, arched his back, and made a caterwauling fit to wake the dead. This was usually enough to see off his rivals.

But not Henderson.

Henderson pounced, tearing a lump from Goliath's ear. For the first time in his adult life, Goliath turned and fled, scuttling indoors through his cat flap, which, even though it was designed for use by a dog, was barely big enough to accommodate him.

Chapter 18

His birth had been a difficult one. He'd emerged feet first and got stuck at his hips.

For a while it had looked as though the infant and his mother were both going to die, so his owner had grabbed hold of his tail, and pulled on it. It didn't seem to make any difference, so he pulled harder, which resulted in the tail being snapped off, leaving the kitten with a tail only about a quarter as long as it should've been.

The owner had next pulled the infant's legs, a tactic which proved to be more successful. The kitten was delivered safely into this world, and his mother miraculously survived the experience.

His owner named him Stump.

Throughout his childhood, Stump had to put up with the rest of the neighbourhood cats laughing at him whenever he ventured out. Perhaps this was why he grew up to be an ill-tempered and vicious brute, who would as soon take off the end of your finger as look at you.

No other cat in Birkby, Huddersfield, would have dared to try to mix it with Goliath when he had been normal, let alone when he'd become a zomcat. But Stump did. Stump soon realised his mistake and turned tail, or such tail as he had, and scuttled home – but not before he'd had an inch of his undersized wagger bitten off by his formidable foe.

Chapter 19

The one that almost got away was called Oscar. He'd lost the lower part of his hind legs in a terrible accident. Fortunately, his owner, who loved him dearly, had been rich, and had paid an engineer to develop a pair of carbon-fibre blades for him. When these were fitted to what remained of his hind legs by a vet, Oscar found he preferred them to the legs he'd lost.

He was, on the whole, a lovely animal, although he had one dreadful character flaw: his vile temper. This had led to him killing Snowball, his cute mate, who'd been white with black patches on her nose and back.

Admittedly, he'd not seen her properly when he'd leapt on her and bit her throat clean through. He'd assumed she was a stranger prowling around his garden, and because he had a short fuse he'd over-reacted. Later, when he realised what he'd done, he'd been heartbroken.

Many was the bird that made the mistake of laughing at Oscar when it took off before he pounced, thinking it'd escaped from his clutches, only to be caught in his jaws seconds later as he sped through the air like a jet-propelled engine of death.

When Henderson leapt at him fully intending to make a fatal attack, Oscar was able to escape by bounding away over fences and privet hedges like some sort of a supercharged jack-rabbit. He did, however, sustain one tiny scratch to his tail, and that was all it took to infect him.

Chapter 20

As dawn broke, eight zomcats made their way silently up the steep slope that led to the top of Stonker Edge: Henderson, Goliath, Stump, Oscar, Tiddles, Sally, Becky and Florence.

They walked at a steady pace to Stonker Edge Farm, and slept together in Hodge's barn.

It became their habit to spend every day sleeping there.

Occasionally they'd wake up during the day, leave the barn, and take a slow walk to a field and back, and sometimes they'd kill and eat a cow, and then they'd curl up in the hay and sleep again.

As dusk fell, the cats would become more alert, and with the onset of night they would venture down into the town of Huddersfield, foraging for food and sex.

Chapter 21

At four in the morning Barbados Jones, a good-natured black man of Afro-Caribbean origin, got out of bed, got his flask ready, and left his small terraced house on Arnold Avenue in Birkby, Huddersfield. He walked down the street heading towards his place of work, a textile factory on Worsted Road. It was the only textile manufacturer left in a town that had once boasted scores of them. He turned a corner and gasped. There, right in front of him, on the gable-end of a house, was a shadow that looked to him to have been cast by a gigantic and terrifying beast.

His eyes followed the legs of the shadow to the base of the wall, then along the pavement to where the beast stood. It was then that he realised it wasn't a terrifying beast at all; it was a domestic cat, albeit one which was rather larger than normal, and rather odd-looking. Its midsection resembled a circular saw. He exhaled and relaxed, and as he was fond of cats, he crouched down and rubbed his fingers together.

"Here, kitty kitty kitty," he said.

The cat looked for a moment as if it was minded to ignore him, but then it padded over. He stroked its cheek and it began to purr. He ran his hand over its back, then stroked it under the chin. The cat's spine was hard as titanium and serrated. The serrations were so sharp that they sliced through the skin on the palm of his hand without him even noticing.

The cat purred more loudly and sniffed Jones's hand and began licking it.

"That tickles," said Jones laughing, unaware that his hand was bleeding, and that the cat was licking the blood trickling from it.

Soon there was no blood left, but the cat was still hungry, so it opened its mouth wide and bit off a chunk of the flesh between Jones's thumb and index finger.

It began chewing it enthusiastically.

"Aaargh!"

Jones held up his hand and looked at it.

"What the, what the..?" He gasped.

Before he could think how to end his question, a number of other cats appeared: Goliath, Stump, Oscar, Tiddles, Sally, Becky and Florence.

Jones looked at them as they advanced. They reminded him of a pride of lions. He retreated, the realisation coming to him that they were hunting for food, and he was the closest thing to a square meal that they could see.

The next thing he knew was blinding pain. Henderson pounced first and the other cats followed, sinking their claws and teeth into his arms, legs, and torso.

Soon all that was left of Barbados Jones was an indistinct bloodstain on the pavement outside number 51, Bleardale Avenue, Birkby, Huddersfield.

Chapter 22

Adrian Broadbent had begun his career in the 1970s as an apprentice TV engineer working for Acme TV Repairs and Rentals (Huddersfield) limited. Colour televisions had swept the nation shortly after he'd been taken on, and the new technology had provided him with an ample supply of work.

He'd shown initiative and had risen to a managerial position with Acme by the end of the eighties.

By the end of the nineties he was running the company. The owner who'd set it up was still there, but he had become little more than a figurehead. It was Adrian who pulled all the strings.

Adrian had done equally well in his personal life. He'd been a good-looking young man, and likeable with it, which meant that he'd been a hit with the many women he met through his extensive social network. He seemed to know all the right things to say to put women at ease, and a good proportion of those he met wanted more from Adrian than small talk.

So he sowed his wild oats, as he described it in the terminology of the time, and at the age of thirty-five, after he felt he'd sown enough of them, he at last married an attractive, intelligent woman ten years his junior, and settled down to a conventional life in Stonker, a posh suburb of Huddersfield at the top of Stonker Edge.

Mr. and Mrs. Adrian Broadbent had been an instant hit on the newly-built housing estate where they'd bought their expensive home. Adrian could tell a tale, and was something of a man's man, despite his way with the ladies. His wife Sandra was bubbly and effervescent, with the result that they were constantly being invited to the dinner parties that were all the rage in those times.

On Saturday afternoons, Adrian would meet a group of his mates in a pub called the Slubber's Arms, and after a couple of pints they'd go to the football ground to watch Huddersfield Town lose, and they'd bemoan the result, and all happily go home to their wives, most of whom had been glad to see the back of them for an hour or two; but not Adrian's wife. She always missed him when he was out of the house, and she was always pleased to see him when he returned.

The couple lived near to the Stonker Edge golf club, which was cheek-by-jowl with Stonker Edge Farm. Adrian fell in with a group of people who played golf, and they encouraged him to take up the game, which he did. He persuaded Sandra to try it, and the couple began playing golf together on Sunday mornings.

The couple's happy existence continued, with the dinner parties and golf being briefly put on hold after the birth of their twin girls. Once the twins were old enough to be left at home with a babysitter, the social life of the Broadbents continued as before.

In the 90's Adrian was able to expand the company and improve his income. He and his wife had bought a house on a large plot, and they had an extension built which gave them two spare bedrooms and a garage big enough to accommodate all five of their cars, plus a home movie theatre. Their movie theatre became a popular feature on the Stonker party scene.

Everyone who met the couple could see that they were happy together, and that they were living the dream.

And they would have been, had Adrian not been harbouring a terrible secret.

It was a secret he dared not share with anyone, particularly his wife, until a certain day dawned.

That was the day that he got to know Paul Formby properly.

Paul Formby was a young apprentice that Adrian had set on at Acme TV Repairs and Rentals (Huddersfield) limited, just as he himself had been set on as an apprentice some twenty-five years previously.

Paul was the opposite of Adrian in many ways: he was a good-looking young man, but shy and reserved, perhaps because he spoke with a lisp. Unlike Adrian, he didn't play the game of being the man's man. He went quietly about his work then stole off home at the end of the day, back to the small terraced house where he lived with his mother.

Adrian often worked late, and sometimes his young apprentice did, too, and Adrian found himself enjoying the times they were alone, discussing their interests after everyone else had left. After a particularly late shift one day, Adrian suggested to Paul that they should go for a pint together. He was delighted when Paul agreed, and also a little guilty, as he suspected that, deep down, he had motives that went beyond mere friendship, but he told himself it was just an innocent drink between mates, or employer and employee, and he'd taken other members of his staff out for the odd beer before, so why not Paul? Anyway, they'd enjoyed a drink together and Paul had gone home, and that was all there was to it. Or so he'd told himself.

But something happened during their meeting that he'd feared for many years. He felt himself getting on so well with Paul that he let his secret slip.

Immediately he'd done so, he regretted it.

That one tiny and almost innocent indulgence with Paul could cause his wife a great deal of misery, if it ever got out.

No more meetings after work with Paul, he told himself.

But he couldn't stick to it, and nor could Paul. And indeed, it soon became apparent that Paul was cut from similar cloth to Adrian.

Chapter 23

It was perhaps inevitable, therefore, that one day Adrian made an excuse to his wife to get away from her for a few hours: he told her he had to stay out all Saturday afternoon on a job. He never went to any job. Instead, he drove to Paul's mother's house, and picked him up. Then he took him to a secret place his wife didn't know about – his allotment on Cemetery Road, in Birkby, Huddersfield.

Adrian's allotment was a curious affair. He'd bought it shortly before he'd married his wife, specifically for the purposes of keeping his activities secret from her. As a result, it wasn't used as an allotment at all. Even though he'd owned it for decades, there were hardly any vegetables growing there. The few that had taken root had done so by accident, having spread onto his plot from the neighbouring allotments.

He'd had a shed built which was like no other. It resembled a house, and was so big that it took up most of the area meant for vegetable-growing activities.

Adrian got out of his car and walked across the soft earth of the allotment to his shed, with Paul following close behind.

Both men felt a thrill of excitement at what was soon to come.

They stopped outside the shed, while Adrian took from his pocket a set of keys and opened the door. They stepped inside, Adrian shut the door behind them, bolted it securely, and locked it with his key for good measure.

"My goodneth," Paul lisped in his gentle voice, "it'th amathing. I wish I had a plathe like thith."

Adrian took his arm, steering the young man towards the end of the shed.

"Look at that in the far pen," he said.

Paul gasped in amazement. What he saw was a thing of beauty.

It was a perfectly white rat twice the size of any rat he'd ever seen before. In the pen with it were several more rats, but they were light grey in colour, and, while big, were small by comparison, being only half again as big as a normal rat.

"I have to keep mine in a little cage in my bedroom," Paul said. "The conditionth are tho cramped. Thometimeth I worry that they don't get to run around enough."

"These pens of mine are very generous, so I don't have that problem," said Adrian. "But I still let them out so that I can play with them."

He looked the younger man in the eye.

"Not a word of this to anyone, you understand. If my wife ever got wind of it, she'd be horrified. Firstly, because she hates rats, and secondly, because if she got to know how much I spend on them every month, she'd go apeshit."

"It'th all right, your thecret'th thafe with me, Adrian. I won't tell a thoul. Can I pick him up, pleathe?"

"Yes, of course. I'll open the door for you."

73

Adrian opened the door of the pen, and the huge white rat came scuttling out, whiskers twitching, his head turning from one man to the other and back again. Paul hesitated and looked at Adrian.

"Go on," said Adrian.

Paul picked up the white rat and held him in his arms.

"He's beautiful," he said.

"And intelligent," said Adrian. "I've been selectively breeding them for generations to make them more intelligent. I swear to God, sometimes I think that the latest lot are as clever as you and I. If only they could speak, they'd be capable of taking over the world."

"He's so friendly."

"Yes, but I'm sure that if someone tried to do anything they shouldn't with him, he'd be more than capable of defending himself, so make sure you handle him gently."

"I will. He theems to underthtand that I'm a friend."

"Yes, he probably does. He has good instincts, and he's very, very bright. He's called Putin, because he's an absolute dictator who rules the rest of them with an iron rod. Let me introduce you to my other friends. Putin, tell them they can come out of the pen."

Putin made a chattering sound with his teeth and the rest of the rats came charging from their pens, crowding around Paul's legs in a friendly grey mass of fur, eyes, and tails.

"Amathing," said Paul. "I've never theen anything like it before. He'th actually communicating with the otherth."

"Yes, and that's not all he can do. I'll show you his other tricks later."

The two men got on so well, and were so fascinated by their pastime, that they didn't notice how much time was passing until daylight turned to dusk.

Adrian looked out of the window.

"I better get you home, Paul," he said. "And I better get home myself. My wife's going to be wondering where I am."

The rats were still all over the floor of the shed, happily sniffing around.

"Putin, tell them it's time for bed now," said Adrian.

Putin made a chattering noise with his teeth.

Instead of going to bed, the rats on the floor launched themselves at Paul and Adrian like a multitude of Excocet missiles, fastening their limpet teeth on the two men. There were hundreds more of the giant rats, they'd been breeding at a faster rate than Adrian had realised, and most of them had been hiding in the hutches he'd built at the back of the pens. Now they came streaming out in a grey-black tide, sweeping quickly across the floor, and enveloping both men.

As he collapsed under the ferocity of their attack, Adrian croaked:

"I told you they were capable of taking over the world. Now it's only a matter of time. Aaargh!"

Paul's answer was monosyllabic.

"Aaaargh!"

The rats feasted well that night. Soon all that was left of the two friends were a few tattered shreds of their clothing, and a polka-dot pattern of bloodstains on the floor of the shed.

Putin led his men back into the pen, to a hole the rats had secretly gnawed in the wall.

The hole led out into the wide world beyond.

It was time to explore, time to conquer.

Their time had come.

Putin and his army were intent on claiming their rightful place at the very top of the food-chain.

Humans would be relegated to the second division, if not the third.

Before Putin got to the hole, something poked through it: a cat's head.

But Putin was no ordinary rat, so he wasn't going to be intimidated by a mere cat.

He was as big as a cat for a start, if not bigger. He was strong, and powerfully built, with a set of incisors so big that they were out of all proportion to his immense head. He leapt at the cat and fastened his teeth into its nose. He was sure the cat would howl with pain, and instantly retreat. He had visions of pursuing it, killing it, and feasting on its blood.

But this cat didn't appear to feel pain. Instead, it became angry. It opened its mouth and hissed. Then it pushed forward. It was too big to squeeze through the hole, but it kept pushing.

Putin held tight onto the cat's nose. He was vaguely aware that something was happening to the wood panelling above the hole. Something seemed to be cutting through it.

There was a rending of wood, a shower of splinters, and something that looked like a very sharp ginger circular sawblade cut through the wooden wall of the shed.

It was then that Putin realised that while he was no ordinary rat, this was no ordinary cat.

With a dismissive swat of his paw, Henderson removed Putin from his snout and pinned him to the floor. Putin squealed and his army of rats rushed forward to defend him.

Henderson bit him in two.

As the rats covered Henderson, fastening their teeth into him, Stump, Oscar, Tiddles, Sally, Becky and Florence entered the shed. Even Goliath was somehow able to squeeze through, although it was a struggle for him to do so.

The zomcats were accompanied by others who'd joined their band: Bernard, Clarence, Fluffy, Puss-Puss, Felix, Tigger, Scoundrel, Macavity, Old Possum, Smokey, Choo-Choo, Olive and a great many more.

Within seconds, the shed was awash with rat-blood.

The global takeover planned by Putin and his band of hyper-intelligent rats had proved to be short-lived. As for the zomcats, they were still hungry after feasting on rat-meat. They went on the prowl around Birkby in search of further sustenance.

Chapter 24

Floyd Rampant made his way through the darkness, followed by Kat De Vine and Gary Fletcher.

Rampant was a celebrity chef who'd been raised from the dead by the same resurrection machine that had been used to raise Henderson the zomcat from the dead. It had turned him into the world's first zombie. He'd created an undead army of celebrity chefs and tried to take over the U.K. He'd also created countless other chef zombies at Chef-Con, the international convention for celebrity chefs. They'd all returned home with plans to take over their own countries.

Rampant's plans to conquer the U.K. had been derailed by the Prime Minister, who had ordered the R.A.F. to drop bombs on Huddersfield while Rampant and his army had been stationed there.

Rampant, De Vine and Fletcher were the only zombies in the U.K. to have survived the bombing.

They'd done so by escaping into the warren of subterranean tunnels that lay hidden beneath the town.

Fletcher caught a rat and gripped it in his hands. It wriggled and kicked, but it couldn't escape. He brought it up to his mouth, bit off its head, and chewed it into a pulp.

"This is disgusting," he said. "I'm fed up of eating rats. When are we going to get any real food?"

Bits of chewed rat head flew from his mouth as he spoke.

The tunnel he and his companions were in was part of a maze which seemed to go on forever, and they could find no way out of it. They'd been down there for months, and the batteries in their torch had long since run out of charge, obliging them to stumble along as best they could in pitch blackness. They'd all lost weight, and were all three of them ravenous even for zombies, who are almost always ravenous.

There was an ominous noise, like an animal in pain.

"What was that?" Kat asked in her husky voice.

"It was my stomach groaning," Fletcher replied. "I can't go on like this for much longer. I need food. I could just go for a bit of prime rump, how about you?"

"I'd love a bit of rump. I'd like it sliced about an inch thick and flash-fried in olive oil with onions and garlic. I'd want the blood to be runny. I hate it when it's overdone. And I'd like it to be sliced from something young, so it's nice and tender."

"You mean like a juicy twenty-year-old student, or something like that?" Fletcher asked, licking his lips.

"Yes, something like that," said Kat. "A student or an apprentice mechanic. I'm quite partial to mechanics."

"I'll tell you another thing," said Fletcher. "I'm gagging for a shag."

"Oh, so am I."

Just then, Rampant stopped.

"Feel that?" He asked.

"What?" Fletcher and Kat asked together.

"That breeze, you silly things," said Rampant in his deceptively effete voice. "We must be near an opening of some kind."

"There's only one opening I want to be near, right now," Fletcher replied, and Kat giggled.

"This is no time for your coarse jokes, Gary," said Rampant. "Now you two concentrate, and follow me."

Rampant felt his way along the wall and turned a corner. The breeze got stronger. He followed the sensation of wind against his face and turned another corner. The ceiling dropped dramatically lower, but he could see light at last. He dropped on all fours and began to crawl. Seconds later, he emerged from under a rock, blinking into the daylight, closely followed by his companions.

They all looked around. They were on the side of a hill. Above them was Stonker Edge, one of the highest points in Huddersfield, and below them was the town itself, sprawled out across the valley, the heart of it a mass of rubble, with tiny people moving amongst the rubble like ants on an anthill.

"Good news," said Rampant. "We're back in Huddersfield, and the British Army has gone home. Look, there's a road down into town over there. We'll get onto it and find a place to hide. Then we'll get hold of some decent two-legged food and do some serious cooking."

Part II: America

Chapter 1

President Doughnut was standing on an elevated wooden platform which was so huge it resembled the deck of a cruise liner. Along its length there was a bandstand, a stage, an al fresco restaurant, and a catering kitchen.

The platform had been erected exactly in the middle of a wall that was sixty-foot-high and nineteen hundred miles long. It was missing one concrete block. Two workers, both undocumented - the American term for what the British would call 'illegal immigrants' - held the missing block aloft and the President applied some mortar to the gap it was meant to occupy, then the illegal, sorry, undocumented, workers carefully positioned it and tapped it into place.

Doughnut turned around. In the distance, he noticed a black car travelling rapidly along the desert road generating clouds of dust in its wake.

On the ground, far below, there was a huge crowd of cheering admirers. He grinned at them. He was wearing a grey suit, white shirt, red tie, and his trademark red baseball cap with the words 'The Doughnut' written across the front. He removed his baseball cap and waved it in the air at the crowd. The crowd was so big that most of the people in it couldn't see him, but they could watch him on the giant screens which were strategically positioned at either end of the wooden platform, and they applauded loudly.

Still grinning, Doughnut spoke to his aide from the corner of his mouth, a gentle Texan breeze disturbing the carefully glued-down strands of his comb-over.

"See that, Tyler?" He said, his words almost drowned out in the noise being generated by the wild applause, "I reckon that's good enough to guarantee me a second term, maybe even a third."

Tyler looked closely at the people below. Many of them were wearing military fatigues, some looked like survivalists, and a small number were dressed in white gowns and pointed hats which resembled the dunce's hats that were, in less enlightened times, forced upon the heads of errant schoolchildren. Here and there, a fiery cross could be seen burning amongst the throng of Doughnut's ecstatic admirers.

"I'm not so sure sir," said the aide. "I'm not convinced that this represents a true cross-section of the American voting demographic."

"For God's sakes Tyler, can't you be happy for me just for once?" Doughnut demanded. "Look at them. Those people love me."

A small group of black protesters appeared on the fringes of the crowd. Doughnut watched as they were hustled away by men in white robes, no-one knows where. He glanced at his watch. "They've been applauding me for one and a half minutes now, and they're still going strong."

After nearly an hour, the applause finally died down. This was the cue for the band that was on the platform with Doughnut to strike up the song "I wish I was in

Dixie", and for the famous singer Ratt Butler to sing it in his fine baritone voice.

As Butler sang the refrain "Look away, look away, look away, Dixieland", Doughnut and his aide walked along the platform to the dining area. Doughnut struggled to keep up with his aide. He was the shortest, fattest president in American history. He was every bit as round as one of the billions of doughnuts sold in his fast food outlets every day, and he was doing his level best to make the entire American nation go the same way.

Their every move was being recorded by a major TV company known as DTV. It was broadcasting the event with a ten-minute time lapse to allow for editing, in case the President made a gaff. The other TV companies had been barred because they all had female reporters whom Doughnut had fallen out with at some time or other.

DTV had cameras set up along the platform with lighting and sound crews. The cameras swivelled to follow Doughnut's progress. He and his aide took their places at the seats that were reserved for them.

The tables were already occupied by dignitaries who included congressmen from the Republican Party and a large number of world leaders. The Queen of England had been invited, but had cried off, citing a prior engagement as the reason, and had sent an obscure relative in her place. At least he was wearing a crown. Doughnut had insisted that any royals who attended the event should wear their crowns, and in the case of the British royals, their ermine as well. Bertie Windsor, the queen's tenth cousin twice removed, was sweating profusely beneath his ermine. At the president's insistence, he was sitting at the top table with him. Everyone else at the table, other than for the British foreign minister and president's aide Tyler, was a C.I.A. security man. The security men were all wearing dark glasses, dark suits, and earpieces with springy cables attached to them. Not one of them so much as cracked a smile.

The British Prime Minister Camemblert had been invited to the event but he'd pulled rank and sent his Foreign Minister instead, somewhat to the President's chagrin.

Still, Doughnut told himself, *at least I've got a Royal here. That's going to be great for my image.*

As soon as Doughnut and Tyler sat down, champagne corks were popped and fizz was handed out amongst the assembled dignitaries.

Bertie looked closely at Doughnut. There was something about Adolf Doughnut's black cowlick of hair and toothbrush moustache that reminded Bertie of someone, but he couldn't think who.

Doughnut took out his mobile phone and held it in front of him, reaching with his free arm around Bertie's royal shoulders.

"Smile, King Bertie," he said. "You're with the President of the United States of America, and we want the world to know how happy you are to be here."

Bertie tightened his lips rather self-consciously into a 'u'-shape, then Doughnut took a selfie of the two of them, and immediately posted it on his Twitter account. Somewhere in a remote White House office, an obscure lackey dreamed up a flattering caption and added it to the selfie.

That should be good for at least another couple of points on the ratings, Doughnut told himself.

The black car that Doughnut had spotted earlier made its way to the wooden platform and pulled up at the front of the crowd. It had the Seal of the President of the United States on the side of it and underneath that were the words 'Presidential Messenger'. The driver climbed out of the car and made his way to the bottom of the steps that led from the ground up to the platform. He was wearing a grey suit and a pained expression. There was a security man at the bottom of the steps. The driver showed the security man an official pass and he was allowed to ascend the staircase. He walked rapidly to the President's table, where he leaned over Doughnut's shoulder.

"Sir," he said. "I'm sorry to disturb you, but I have something you should see. It's an urgent message from the President of Mexico."

The Mexican president was one of the few world leaders who wasn't attending Doughnut's topping-out ceremony. He hadn't given any reason for his non-attendance; he hadn't even replied to his invitation.

Doughnut nodded and the messenger handed him a brown envelope.

Doughnut opened the envelope and frowned. There was a bill in it. It was the bill for the 50 billion dollar cost of building the wall. Doughnut had sent the bill to the

Mexican president. He wondered why it'd been sent back to him. Doughnut would have understood if the Mexican president had simply ignored the bill, but not this. It didn't make sense. He turned the bill over. His frown deepened. There was writing on the reverse. The Mexican president had scrawled the words "Fuck you Gringo" on the back of the bill.

Bertie saw the bill in Doughnut's hands and read the words at the same time as the President did.

"I didn't know your name was Gringo," he said.

The president quickly thrust the bill into the pocket of his suit trousers.

"That God-damned wetback bastard," he muttered under his breath. Then he turned to Bertie.

"It's not," he said. "Gringo is the name of the pet cat we keep in the White House. Sometimes he receives hate mail from cat-haters. You know how some people are."

"Cripes," said Bertie. "Cat-haters, eh? You wouldn't think that anyone could possibly hate cats. They're so cute and fluffy."

Just then one of the security men pressed his earpiece further into his ear. He was maintaining a grim facial expression, the way he'd been trained to do at the C.I.A. headquarters in Fairfax. He adjusted his facial expression from grim to seriously grim and stood up. He looked through his dark glasses at his colleagues and nodded at two of them, who also stood up. The three of them walked to the wall and looked over it onto the Mexican side. Two of them stayed by the wall; the third returned to the table. He bent over and whispered into Doughnut's ear.

"Excuse me, Mr. President, there's something you need to see," he said.

"Can't it wait?" Doughnut asked impatiently. "I'm talking to the Queen of England."

"It's a Code Red, Mr. President," said the security man.

The president dabbed at his lips with a napkin to remove some drops of champagne from them, then he pushed his chair back so he could extricate his massive belly from under the table. He struggled to his feet.

"All right," he said. "Whatever this is, it better be important."

"It is. Follow me, sir," said the security man. He led Doughnut to where he'd left his two C.I.A. colleagues, who were still looking over the wall.

"Take a look, sir."

Doughnut had to stand on tiptoe to look, because he was rather short. He peered over the wall. On the other side, he saw a mass of Mexicans milling about at the bottom of the wall. Some of those at the back were carrying ladders. There were more ladders amongst the mass of Mexicans that were being passed overhead from the rear of the crowd to the front. When the ladders reached the front of the crowd, those in the vanguard placed them against the wall. As Doughnut watched, several Mexicans began to climb up the ladders. There was something about them that was rather threatening.

The leading Mexican was just below the point where Doughnut was sticking his head over the wall. He looked ravenous, and his skin was yellow. He opened his mouth to reveal a set of sharp teeth and he reached up as if to grab Doughnut, but that wasn't possible, as the top of his ladder stopped short a good distance below the top of the wall.

"Good job we built the wall so high, sir," said the security man.

Doughnut, who was shaken by what he'd seen, stepped back.

"Yes," he said. "Yes, it is. Those things are not just Mexicans. Who – who - or what, are they?"

"Zombies, sir. They're zombies."

"Zombies?" Doughnut asked in disbelief. "Zombies don't exist. They can't. They're fictional creations you only get in books and films."

"That's what we thought, sir. But then we heard rumours through our intel gathering at Fairfax and we began to investigate. We sent you some reports about it. We warned you that the Mexicans might have a plague of zombies on their hands, but this is the first time we've had a confirmed sighting."

"Zombies," Doughnut said again, pulling himself together. "What do we pay you people for, over at the C.I.A.? This is the biggest pile of horse manure you've come up with since the Bay of Pigs fiasco."

"Take another look, sir."

The President leaned over the top of the wall again, peering more closely at the slavering face below him.

"My God, you're right. They *are* zombies," he said. "It's a good job I had this wall built."

"It's only a matter of time before they get some longer ladders sir. Then they'll be able to get over the top."

Doughnut didn't hear those words because his mind was racing. He was remembering something about zombies. What was it? Oh yes, it was a telephone call he'd received from some limey or other. How long ago had that been? He couldn't remember. It could've been weeks or it could've been months. Anyway, this limey had claimed he was from the British Foreign and Commonwealth Department or something like that, and he'd said there was a worldwide epidemic of celebrity chef zombies and they all had to have their brains blown out.

Doughnut knew all about the weird limey sense of humour and he'd treated the whole thing as a joke. He'd assumed that a practical joker in England had rung him up and tried to get him to do something stupid to discredit himself. But now he realised the telephone call had been for real. He shifted uneasily from one foot to the other, remembering the intel reports from the C.I.A. that he'd never bothered to read, some of which had had the word 'zombie' on the front, which he'd taken at the time to be a code word for the ruined economy of a small country he'd invaded. *Maybe I should've at least skimmed through those reports,* he said to himself.

"Sir, Mr. President Sir! It's only a matter of time before they get some longer ladders and then they'll be able to get over the top."

The President emerged from his reverie and this time he heard what the CIA man was telling him.

There's still time to extricate myself from this disaster, he thought. *I just have to finish the topping-out ceremony without any of it coming to light, and then I can get some-one to clear up the mess when there's no-one around to see what's going on.*

"How long have we got?" He asked.

"Two hours, maybe three. Longer if we get our marks-men to start picking them off"

"Hold your fire for now. We don't want to worry our guests, and we don't want anyone to know there might be a problem with the wall. Get the waiters to bring the mains out straight after the starters, and the puddings out straight after the mains. That way we'll get through the meal quickly. As soon as people finish eating, get them packed off to their hotels in their official cars. Another thing. Get that band to play all their songs up-tempo, at least twice as quick as they should be played, and don't let them stop the music until they're told; and don't start shooting until all the guests have left. Have you got all that?"

"Yes, sir."

Doughnut went back to his seat and nonchalantly tucked into his starter as soon as it arrived.

"That was jolly good," said Bertie when he'd cleared his plate. "I could do with a nice relaxing break now, for fifteen minutes or so, before the main course arrives."

No sooner had the words left his mouth than the main course was placed in front of him.

"Cripes," he said. "That was quick." He turned to Doughnut. "But that's you Americans all over, isn't it? You like to have everything quick, don't you?"

"Not everything" said Doughnut, thinking of the gorgeous pouting twenty-five-year-old Eastern European girlfriend he had waiting for him back in his hotel suite. They were going to get married soon, and when they did, she'd be coming with him to engagements like this one as his First Lady.

Bertie ate rapidly, the high-speed music somehow forcing him to swallow without chewing anything. A waiter who was hovering behind Bertie snatched his dinner plate away as soon as he'd polished off the last morsel of steak from it. A second waiter deposited a piping hot pudding in front of him before he'd had the chance to dab the gravy from his lips with his napkin. He looked around to make sure the president was eating and when he saw that he was, Bertie followed suit.

In no time at all, the three-course meal, which had been scheduled to last for over two and a half hours, ended to the "William Tell Overture". At the same time, the limousines for the dignitaries began to form a line at the bottom of the wooden platform.

Doughnut got to his feet to tell everyone to proceed to their cars in an orderly fashion. Just as he opened his mouth to speak, the first wave of zombies made it over the wall, having got hold of longer ladders quicker than anyone would have thought possible. The TV crews had their backs to the wall, as they were intent on recording every second of the topping-out ceremony. Consequently, they were unaware of the danger coming at them from the other side. Within seconds they were overwhelmed, without having had the chance to film a single second of zombie action to broadcast to the nation. The zombies pulled the plug on the power to their equipment, to prevent news of their onslaught getting out.

The wave of undead Mexicans moved swiftly forwards.

Chapter 2

The C.I.A. men immediately interposed themselves between the president and the zombies and began shooting. A hail of lead whined through the air, tearing into the undead flesh of the zombies without stopping them.

When they heard gunfire and saw zombies, many of the women began screaming their heads off. So did some of the younger men, who, unlike older generations, hadn't been brought up to behave like real men.

International politicians, businessmen, and heads of state panicked when they heard the screaming and got up to rush in all directions, colliding with one another and turning over tables and chairs in their haste. The orchestra, having been told it was their duty to perform until ordered to stop by the C.I.A., continued to play. They struck up "I'm going Home to Dixie" as chaos spread like a forest fire across the deck of the wooden platform. All-in-all, it was a scene that resembled the deck of the Titanic just before it sank.

The first wave of zombies rapidly overwhelmed the C.I.A. men and got in and amongst the melee of panic-stricken dignitaries and overturned dining furniture.

Tyler grabbed Doughnut's arm and dragged him from the platform towards his car.

Doughnut heard a posh British voice.

"Cripes, you look a bit off-colour. Aaaaargh!"

He glanced back just in time to see a set of zombie teeth sinking into Bertie's pale throat. As Bertie lacked any sort of a chin, it was relatively easy for the zombie to target his huge Adam's apple and rip it out. Blue blood fountained from Bertie's mortal wound into the air and joined the common blood of the many other guests caught up in the general melee.

"This way, sir," said Tyler, propelling Doughnut to the safety of his official limousine and quickly following behind him.

When they were both in the back seat of the car, Tyler slammed the door shut.

"Albuquerque!" He shouted to the driver. "And step on it!"

The driver put his foot on the gas and sped off into the desert of New Mexico with his passengers.

Doughnut looked out of the rear windscreen and watched as a band of survivalists and Klan members charged up the staircase to the platform to teach the zombies a lesson for disrupting their hero's party. They soon found their way into cooking pots in the vast catering kitchen that the platform had been equipped with, which the zombies had requisitioned within minutes of eliminating the presidential bodyguards.

When the carnage of the topping-off ceremony was far behind him, Doughnut switched on the presidential television in his limo and began searching for news of the disaster that had overwhelmed his topping-out ceremony. There was none. All he could find were advertisements promoting himself, Adolf 'The Doughnut' Doughnut and his achievements as President, or his one achievement, which was building a bloody big wall.

"Why can't I find any news, God-dammit?" he growled as he flipped channels in quick succession and saw only more and more images of himself wearing his bright-red baseball cap.

"It's because you bought up all the air time sir, remember?" Said Tyler.

Then Doughnut did remember. The main reason he'd won the election was because he was the richest man on the planet. So, rich, in fact, that he'd been able to purchase all the available air time on all the TV channels in America and strangle the life out of the campaigns of all of his rivals.

After he'd been elected, he'd bought another big tranche of air time just to make sure he remained in the public eye and his ratings didn't slip. So much air time was now devoted to promoting the president that very little was left over for legitimate programming, even the news.

"Now I do remember," Doughnut replied. "Maybe it's just as well I did that. It means we can release information about what went on back there in our own time, the way we want to release it. Get that organised for me, Tyler."

"Yes, sir, Mr. President."

"And make sure no-one gets to know that a bunch of zombies was able to climb over that wall we just spent fifty billion bucks of taxpayer dollars on. If that news were to get out I'd be finished."

"Yes, sir, Mr. President."

"And tell the Pentagon to deal with those Mexican chef zombies or whatever the hell they are. Tell them to make sure that no more of them get over that wall. And another thing, and this is probably the most important thing you have to do today Tyler. I need you to come up with a plan to cover this mess up for me. Cover it up and completely bury it so that no-one ever gets to hear about it."

"Will that be all Mr. President?"

"That'll be all for now, Tyler."

As the car sped through the desert, Tyler got on the phone and made numerous calls. He then logged onto the presidential internet connection and sent a tranche of emails to see that the president's instructions were carried out.

Doughnut, meanwhile, wondered how he'd put a positive spin on things if word got out that his wall had proved ineffective against wetback zombies using nothing more sophisticated than ladders to climb over it.

The thought made him tense. How can I relax? He asked himself. Then he thought of his young girlfriend in his Albuquerque hotel suite.

When they got to the hotel, Doughnut's girlfriend met him in the lobby and he took her arm.

"We need some private time together, babe," he said, steering her towards the lift.

She assumed the smile she'd become expert at, the one that hid what she was thinking, and feeling, and allowed herself to be led by Doughnut into the lift, out of it, and into their suite.

"What's the matter with you, honey? Are you tense again? Because if you are, don't worry, I know how to relax you."

She began to peel off her clothes and so did Doughnut.

A short while later he was lying on the hotel bed next to her, flushed and satisfied.

"That was great babe. You've gotta excuse me. We can have dinner together later."

"That's all right. Don't rush back on my account."

He dressed quickly as his girlfriend got into the shower. He called his aide.

"Tyler, get up here. I need you to brief me on what's going on about that mess back there with the wall."

Tyler made his way to the President's luxurious hotel suite.

"All right," said Doughnut, as soon as Tyler walked through the door. "Give me the low-down on what you've done. I want to know everything."

The two men stood together in the middle of the room and Tyler began.

"I've organised a complete news blackout on the topping-out ceremony, sir," he said. "I justified it as being in the interests of national security. But that won't bury the story. We need to be able to explain why all those camera crews and the rest of them never made it home. So I've been in touch with the C.I.A. about it. They've organised an air crash on the wall. That will simultaneously wipe out the zombies and provide us with an explanation for why those people disappeared. As far as the networks are concerned, the DTV news broadcast went off air because of the plane crash. Maybe it won't completely stack up, but we'll probably be able to sell it anyway. We just have to hope to God that no-one had the chance to catch any of it on a mobile phone and get it on the internet."

"Good work, Tyler."

"I think we should involve the Pentagon as well as the C.I.A. We may need to send in the marines, in case there are some zombie air-crash survivors who need to be suppressed."

"Don't tell me about it Tyler, just do it. I need deniability, so you shouldn't be telling me these things. I don't want to hear anything that might incriminate me, if there's an inquiry later. You should know that by now."

Tyler nodded.

"Consider it done, sir."

"Another thing, get onto the C.I.A. again, and find out if those Mexican zombies aren't the only ones we've got to deal with. Tell them to find out if we've got a zombie problem here in the U.S. of A. I want them to concentrate on chefs. Celebrity chefs. Get the low-down on 'em. I've been hearing rumours."

"What kind of rumours, Mr. President?"

"The rumour kind of rumour, God-dammit! I don't have to explain myself to you, Tyler. You're my aide, not some snotty female limey interviewer from the BBC."

"Very good, Mr. President. Er, did you say celebrity chefs?"

"That's exactly what I said, Tyler. Now get onto it right away."

Forty-eight hours later, Tyler hurried along the White House the corridor leading to the Oval office.

"I have a report for you, Mr. President," he said when he got there. "It's from the C.I.A. I think you ought to look at it right away."

Doughnut, who was standing next to his desk practising his golf swing, lowered his club and glared at his aide.

"God-dammit Tyler," he said. "What's the matter with you? Can't you see I'm busy? Put it on my desk. I'll look at it later."

The President raised his golf club again and wiggled his backside.

Tyler stepped forward and put the report on Doughnut's desk.

"Now you've made my desk untidy. Can't you find somewhere else to put it?"

Tyler waved the report around uncertainly as he tried to decide where it should go. Eventually he said:

"You really should read it right away, sir, it's important."

Doughnut lowered his golf club again.

"Just tell me what it says. I've got to practice my swing. I've arranged a round of golf with the Veep this afternoon, and I don't want that sonofabitch to give me another licking."

"It says those rumours you heard were correct sir. We do have a plague of celebrity chef zombies on our hands, here in the United States."

Doughnut dropped his golf club to the floor.

This was news he'd been dreading.

Chapter 3

"We have to do something about these Zombie *sono-fabitches* before the problem gets out of hand, but what?"

"The C.I.A. recommends that we get the military onto it."

"That's out of the question. We need to keep a lid on this thing. If we send troops into our cities, everyone will know about it. We've got to keep our operation low profile."

"I think we should follow the C.I.A.'s advice, sir."

"The C.I.A. is as good as advising me to throw away the next election. I'm not going to do that. Let me think. I've got it. Find me someone who can get rid of the zombies on the quiet. Someone so good he can take care of this problem on his own. What I want is a one-man army. Go and find me a one-man army."

"Yes sir, Mr. President."

That afternoon, when Doughnut got back from his round of golf with the Vice-President, Tyler was waiting for him at the magnificent front door of the White House.

Doughnut climbed from his chauffeur-driven limo with a golf club in his hand.

"Get my golf bag from the back of the car, Tyler," he said.

Tyler reached into the back of the limo and got the bag, slung it over his shoulder, and walked by Doughnut's side into the White House, down its long central corridor.

Doughnut was wearing a green visor, a green short-sleeve shirt, and pants with a loud checked pattern on them. He was carrying one of his golf clubs, swinging it as he walked.

"That ass-hole of a Vice-President of mine almost cheated me out of a win," he said.

"Sir, I've found someone to take care of the zom-"

"Are you listening to me, Tyler? I said that sonofabitch the Vice-President almost cheated me out of a win. He lost his ball in the rough twice, and both times he said he'd found it. But it couldn't have been where he said it was. He moved the God-damned thing both times. I've got a good mind to sack him and get someone else to do his job. Better still, I'll do it myself. I might as well. He's no damned good at it anyway."

"That's a great idea Mr President. By the way, you might like to know that I've found someone to take care of the zombies. He's called Macho Havoc."

"What's that? What are you babbling on about, Tyler? Macho what?"

"Macho Havoc, sir."

"What in God's name is that?"

"It's not what, it's who, sir. Macho Havoc is the man you asked for. He's the best there is. He's a regular one-man army."

As they proceeded further along the corridor they came to a door on the right that had a sign on it: 'Male Toilets'.

"Follow me, Tyler."

Doughnut opened the door to the male toilets and they both went in.

Oh please, thought Tyler. *Not this, not again. Anything but this, please God.*

It was one of the smaller sets of toilets in the White House; it only had ten cubicles in it. Doughnut selected the cubicle that had the word 'President' on the door and pushed it open.

"Hold this for me," Doughnut said, handing his golf-club to Tyler.

He left the door wide open and entered the cubicle while droppping his pants. Tyler moved to one side so that he couldn't see into it.

"Tyler, where the hell are you?" Doughnut demanded. "I can't see you."

Tyler moved so that he was in full view of Doughnut again. He tried not to look as uncomfortable as he felt, while the president lowered himself onto the toilet seat.

"What do we know about this Havoc character?" Doughnut asked.

Tyler hoped he'd be able to leave soon. He spoke faster than usual.

"He's Ex-Special Forces, ex-Navy Seal, and ex-C.I.A. There's not a trouble spot in the world he hasn't been to, at some time or other."

"Slow down, will you? I can hardly tell what you're saying."

"He's a fine man, Mr. President. If anyone can do this on his own, Havoc can."

Doughnut's face reddened. Tyler felt himself shudder. He held his breath.

"What are you waiting for? NNNggggg. Get him hired. Nnnng."

"YessirMrPresident."

Tyler left the toilets as quickly as he could.

When he was outside in the corridor, and could breathe properly again, he took out his mobile phone and punched in a number.

"Is that Mr. Havoc? It is? Good. No, you don't know me. We haven't spoken before. I'm Brett Tyler, the President's aide. That's right, the president of the United States of America. No, it's no joke. You can check up on me if you like. The president has an important job for you. A wet job. Several wet jobs, in fact. No, I can't provide photographs, but they won't be necessary. I'll be able to give you enough information without the need for photographs. Your instructions are to be given by verbal briefing only, nothing in writing. It might be best if we were to meet up. How quickly can you get up to Washington? Okay, good, we'll meet in a bar I know. The Smith Commons on H Street. I'll be on the second floor, and I'll be carrying a copy of the Washington Post. I'll be wearing a blue tie and drinking a cocktail. What's that you say? Don't bother? You'll just look me up on the presidential website. Oh, I see what you mean. Of course you will. All right, I'll see you tomorrow at 2.30 p.m."

The next day, Tyler went to the second floor of the Smith Commons in a state of some trepidation. He had no idea what to expect of the man he was due to meet. Havoc was known only by reputation; there were no pictures of him anywhere, and as far as Tyler could tell, no-one he knew had met him. But military men he respected told tales of Havoc's exploits, which sounded superhuman. So, he had no doubt that Havoc was his man.

The second floor of the Smith Commons was like the lounge of a private house, only far bigger. Tyler bought a bottle of Bud and found a nice spot where he could be on his own, propping up the bar. He stood with his back to it and positioned himself so that he could see the door and keep tabs on everyone who entered. There was no-one within ten yards of him. No one in front of him; no-one to either side of him; and to his rear was the solid edge of the bar, which he could feel against his back.

He took a sip of his Bud then lowered his glass.

That was when the impossible happened.

Chapter 4

A deep, menacing voice whispered in his ear:

"You're the fella who called me about a job, ain't ya?"

Tyler started.

He could have sworn there was no-one nearby. He turned to look at his interlocutor, and what he saw amazed him. There, right next to him, was a man so big that Tyler couldn't possibly have missed him, but missed him he had.

The man was African-American, shaven-headed, six feet four inches tall, and, even though he was wearing a jacket, obviously well-muscled, but not like a bodybuilder. These were the muscles of a fighter, no, a finely-tuned killing machine. Tyler shuddered. He got the impression that his new acquaintance would kill anyone in an instant if he took against them.

"What's the matter, son?" The man asked, in a slow drawl that sounded as if it had been forged in the voodoo region of the Mississippi Delta. "Cat got yo' tongue?"

"No," said Tyler, "No, sorry. I was taken aback, that's all. I didn't see you coming."

"Nobody ever does, son."

"I suppose I ought to be pleased to hear that. What would you like to drink?"

The man raised his right hand. There was a glass tumbler in it containing two fingers of whiskey.

"I'm partial to a fine bourbon, but I've already gotten one, thank you kindly. Now how's about we find somewhere nice and quiet, and you tell me what this business with the president is all about."

Havoc motioned with his head and set off walking. Tyler followed him to a dark corner where Havoc put his drink down on a table.

"You put yo' drink next to mine, Mr. Tyler," he said.

Tyler did as he was told.

Without asking for permission, Havoc began to pat him down.

"Just a routine precaution, Mistah Tyler," Havoc said as he did it. "I wouldn't want to be having a private discussion here with you, without checking first that you aren't all wired up and sharing our discussion with yo' friends back in the White House, or over in Fairfax. Much as I admire those good ol' boys, I wouldn't trust a single one of 'em as far as I could throw a fresh turd into a high wind."

Havoc's unusually large hands made short work of the pat-down.

"Looks like yo' all clear, Mistah Tyler," he said. "Now you tell me some more 'bout this business you want to transact."

Tyler glanced around the interior of the bar. There was no-one within earshot, and the background music and murmur of conversation could be relied upon to drown out anything that he and Havoc discussed. This was one of the reasons he'd chosen the place, but by no means the only reason. Nevertheless, Tyler lowered his voice as he spoke.

"The business concerns chefs," he said. "We want you to dispose of all the high-profile chefs in the country. The ones you might call 'celebrity chefs'."

"Is that some kind of a code you talkin' boy? When you is sayin' 'celebrity chefs' to me, do you really mean somethin' else? 'Cause if you do, there ain't nobody told me the code just yet."

"It isn't code, Mr. Havoc. We really do want you to – er - remove our celebrity chef problem."

"What problem you talking 'bout Mistah Tyler? Because from where I'm standing, I don't see no problem with chefs whether they're celebrities or just the regular kind of chefs. So why fo' you askin' me to get rid of yo' chef problem? It don't make any sense to me."

"Can't you just do the job, Mr. Havoc?"

"If it was a normal job, then I'd do it Mistah Tyler, and I wouldn't ask any questions. Let's say fo' instance, if you asked me to kill a terrorist, I'd do it. Iffen you asked me to rescue one of our boys when he was in trouble, I'd do it. If you told me to shove a fresh turd down the throat of someone you heard bad mouthin' the American flag, I'd do it. But I'm not killin' any chefs fo' you, unless you tell me why for you wantin' those chefs dead."

Tyler cleared his throat. He glanced around the bar again.

"It's because they aren't ordinary chefs anymore, Mr. Havoc," he said. "Something's happened to them."

"What's happened boy? Get to the point. I'm getting mighty sick of standing here listenin' to yo' mouth flapping and not tellin' me anything."

Tyler moved closer to Havoc, so close that they were almost touching.

"They've all turned into zombies," he whispered.

"You better speak up Mistah Tyler, because I'm not hearing you right. For a moment there, I thought you said zombies."

"I did. That's exactly what I said. Zombies."

Havoc turned away.

"What are you doing?"

"I'm leaving Mistah Tyler. I'm not wasting any mo' of my time."

Tyler grabbed Havoc's muscular upper arm. Havoc looked at him and Tyler felt as if fingers of ice were gripping his heart. He let go.

"Wait, please. Just give me two minutes to explain."

"Two minutes is all you got then I'm out of here."

"All right. It's crazy, but it's true. You know that plane crash that wrecked the president's wall and killed all those dignitaries at the topping-out ceremony? It was staged. The plane was deliberately crashed there, after everyone had been killed, to cover up the evidence of what had really gone on."

"And what did go on, Mr. Tyler?"

"There was an attack by zombies from the other side of the border. They were mainly Mexican celebrity chef zombies. Don't believe me? Here's some film taken from a drone we sent overhead to record what was happening just before we crashed the plane."

He held up his cell phone. Havoc narrowed his eyes into slits and looked at the screen.

"That don't prove nuthin'. You could fake that even easier than you could fake a plane crash."

"What if I could prove it?"

"Just how you gonna prove a thing like that?"

"I could take you to meet one of those things, a zombie chef, if you'll let me."

Tyler swallowed hard. He'd hoped he wouldn't have to go to such lengths to get Havoc onside. And beyond showing Havoc what a zombie chef looked like, he didn't have any sort of a plan. He could only hope that it panned out all right for them both.

"Well now, you've got me right intrigued Mistah Tyler. Here was I, thinkin' you was joshin' me around in some way, and now you're saying you can show me a real live – excuse me, – dead, zombie. This I gotta see. I'm gonna put my plans to leave on hold, till you've shown me this zombie of yours. Where you gonna take me?"

"Nowhere. We don't have to go anywhere. There's one working in the kitchen here, right now. He's a guest chef. They've brought him in from Baltimore. He's got his own radio show. I've got it on good authority from the C.I.A. that he's part of the zombie plot."

"You never mentioned no plot to me, befo'."

"Well, there is a plot. They're planning to take over. Not just the restaurants, either. They want control of everything, including you and me. Anyway, one of them is busy cooking the food today. He's a celebrity chef called Skipper Lee. Are you armed?"

"Why fo' would I need to be armed Mistah Tyler?"

"You don't know what these things are like. I've seen them in action."

"Well, I ain't brought no big gun with me, if that's what you mean. I've just got a little itty-bitty sidearm under my jacket. It's hardly what I'd call being armed, but it'll have to do."

Tyler wasn't sure he felt reassured by that. He'd seen what zombies were capable of. He'd seen them walk through gunfire without flinching.

"That gun of yours might buy us time. That's all it'll do. I want you to know that, before we meet him. Now we have to find an excuse to go into the kitchen."

"We don't need no excuse. We can just walk right in there."

Tyler remembered the scenes of horror at the topping out ceremony. An unwelcome image came to his mind, of vicious yellowing teeth sinking into the pale neck of Bertie Windsor, the 43rd person in line to the British throne. He shuddered at the recollection, and realised that he wasn't prepared to confront Skipper Lee. When he'd dreamed up the idea, he hadn't given sufficient thought to the dangers. Now that the idea was close to becoming a reality, he was all too aware of the risk he'd be taking, and he didn't want to take it. He wanted to go home.

"Won't that look a bit odd?" He asked, playing for time.

"Every damn thing that's happened since I walked in here has been odd. One more odd thing ain't gonna make a blind bit of difference. We're just gonna go on a walk right into that kitchen. Then you're gonna confront that chef fellow, Skipper Lee, and tell him what y'all think of him, and we'll see how he likes them apples."

"I don't think I can do that."

"Why not?"

"I don't think he'll like them apples one bit, and I'm scared. I'm too scared to go in there and confront a zombie. I've seen them in action."

Havoc smiled.

"Don't you worry Mistah Tyler, I got the cure for that."

"Cure?"

"That's right, I said cure. I can make it so you don't worry about that zombie feller one little bit, no, sir. I can make it so that you'll just go walking right into that there kitchen and you won't give so much as a flying turd about that Skippoh Lee feller you is gettin' yourself all worked up about."

"How will you do that?"

"I'm just going to give you a sense of what yo' priorities are, Mistah Tyler."

"What do you mean?"

"Here, let me show you."

Havoc gripped Tyler by the throat. His hand was so big that Tyler imagined Havoc's finger and thumb meeting each other around the back of his neck. He tried to yell to attract the attention of the other customers in the bar, but the pressure of on his throat made any form of speech, or even sound, impossible.

A man who was standing nearby saw what was happening. Havoc gave him a threatening glance – one glance was all it took - and the man quickly looked away. A couple of the other customers made the mistake of looking their way and wished they hadn't done, when Havoc gave them his gamma-ray glare.

"Now in case you still don't know what yo' priorities are, Mr. Tyler, I'm going to spell them out fo' you, nice and simple, to make sure you understand 'em. Your main priority is to be scared of me. So scared of me, in fact, that you ain't gonna have room in yo' fear box to be scared of anythin' else. That's also yo' last priority and ever-thing in between. You got that, Mistah Tyler?"

Tyler thought he was going to die, here, in a packed bar, in front of a crowd of people, none of whom seemed minded to help.

He tried to say 'Yes, I've got it,' but all he could do was gasp like a landed fish.

Havoc smiled again.

"You know something? I think we're beginning to understand each other. It's a mighty fine thing, when a man can say he understands his fellow man. That's why I'm feeling so danged happy all of a sudden."

He drew Tyler closer and raised him up until their noses were almost touching.

"We do understand each other, now, don't we?" He asked, relaxing his grip slightly so that Tyler was just about able to answer.

"Yes. Oh yes, we do. We do understand each other. I understand you as well as any one man could possibly understand another man. My understanding of you is complete. It lacks nothing."

Havoc let Tyler go, and Tyler landed with a bump on the floor.

"I'm mighty pleased to hear that. If there's one thing that riles me, it's being misunderstood. Now you just walk over to that kitchen door, open it, and walk right in. I'll be right behind you."

"What then?"

Havoc gripped him by the throat again.

"I'm disappointed in you, Mistah Tyler. You said you understood me. I'm gonna let go of yo' throat, and you ain't gonna ask any mo' damn fool questions. Is that clear?"

Tyler was just about able to nod.

"Right then, we'll start again from where we were."

Havoc set him back on the floor.

"Get yo' ass into that kitchen."

Tyler walked like a condemned man. Despite what Havoc had said and done, he was still scared of the zombie. But there was something about Havoc, he had to admit to himself, that made him even scarier than a zombie, if that was possible. But in any event, it was academic. Tyler was certain that if he didn't do what he'd been told to do, Havoc would kill him; if not now, then later. The man was a killing machine. There was no other way to describe him.

Tyler walked towards the door at the end of the bar, the one that kept opening and shutting as waiters went in and out of the kitchen that lay behind it. The meals they were carrying looked more than appetising – they looked delicious. It seemed that Skipper Lee could still cook, even if he was a zombie.

They were no more than a yard from the door when it opened, a cloud of steam wafted from the kitchen, and a waiter emerged from the cloud. Tyler paused to let the waiter go past. Just as the door was about to close, Havoc stepped forward and held it open. He didn't have to say anything. Tyler went through the doorway with the look of a man walking to the gallows.

Everything behind that door was hectic. There were a dozen sous chefs at work, filling the air with the clattering of crockery and steel, the bubbling of pans on hobs, and the chopping of cleavers.

In the background, a chef with a bigger chef's hat than the rest of them were wearing, directed operations.

Tyler turned to Havoc.

"That's him."

"Keep right on walking. Ain't no point in stopping now."

They pushed their way past the sous chefs and headed through the vast kitchen towards Skipper lee. Lee saw them and frowned. He was a big man, paunchy but well-muscled, like a heavyweight powerlifter. Tyler stopped in front of Lee, a good arm's length away, and then some. Havoc stood beside him.

"What are you doing in my kitchen?" Lee asked.

"Don't you have something to say to Mistah Lee, Tyler?"

"Say? Me? I'm not sure what you mean."

"It seems like yo' getting plumb forgetful. You better get yo' memory back right quick, or I'll be obliged to give you some assistance in the memory department that you won't much care to receive. Am I making myself clear?"

"Yes, very clear."

Lee folded his arms, cocked his head to one side, and glared at Tyler.

The sous chefs took no notice. Visitors were their boss's concern, not theirs, and besides, they were too busy to be bothered about anything other than cooking.

"The thing is, Mr. Lee," Tyler said, "that, well, how could I put this, I have reason to believe, good reason, based on more than mere spec-"

"Spit it out, God-damn you, Tyler, before I treat you to a freshly-made knuckle sandwich."

Tyler composed himself.

"We know you're a zombie, Mr. Lee."

Lee tilted his head back while raising his eyebrows.

"You know I'm a what?" He asked.

"A zombie."

"Ha ha ha ha ha. Whatever next. Ha ha ha ha ha. Who told you tha-ha ha ha."

He wiped tears from the corners of his eyes.

"You sayin' you ain't no zombie, Mistah Lee?"

Lee unfolded his arms and spread them wide.

"I'm saying I've never heard anything so preposterous in my entire life," he said. "Zombie. As if. Your friend has been reading too many comic books. Isn't it past his bedtime?"

Havoc took a step closer to Lee.

"Well now, if you ain't no zombie, you won't mind me doing a test to make sure, will you? 'Cause you ain't got nuthin' to lose if I do."

He grabbed the chef's wrist with his left hand. It felt slippery, as if it had a coating on it of some kind. He pulled it. Lee attempted to jerk his hand free of Havoc's grip. Not successfully. As if from nowhere, a knife appeared in Havoc's right hand.

"Why fo' you struggling, Mistah Lee? I ain't gonna hurt you. This here knife is so sharp, I'll be able to cut yo' hand, and you won't even feel it. And when I see if red blood comes outa that cut, that's when I'll know which one o' you fellas is telling the truth."

Lee jerked his arm, much harder this time, and freed it from Havoc's grip.

Havoc glanced at his own hand. His black skin had a coating of white makeup on it; the skin on Lee's wrist, which had been concealed by the makeup, was exposed to view. It was yellow.

"Now what you done that fo', Mistah Lee?"

"I'm not letting you cut me. What do you take me for? I've answered your damn fool questions. Now get out of here, before I call security and have you thrown out."

A smile played on Havoc's lips.

When Tyler had told him that Skipper Lee was a zombie, he'd been incredulous. He'd insisted on a showdown with Lee, to punish Tyler for his lies. When he'd met Lee, Havoc had instinctively felt that there was something odd about him. And now that he'd seen the deathly yellow skin that lay beneath Lee's makeup, Havoc had almost become a believer in zombies himself.

He raised his arms slightly, as if in supplication. He still had the knife in his right hand.

"Now let's not be hasty," he said. "There ain't no need for any unpleasantness with any security men. We were just goin', weren't we, Tyler?"

"We were? Oh yes, of course we were."

Just as the words were leaving Tyler's mouth, Havoc moved forward with a speed that took both Tyler and Lee by surprise. He made a short slicing movement with the knife, carving an incision down the back of Lee's left hand. Lee didn't flinch. He looked at the incision then held the back of his hand up before his eyes, scowling at it. He turned it so that the palm was facing his face.

Havoc and Tyler could both now see the back of Lee's hand clearly. The incision was a deep one, and the skin was parted at either side of it, so that it looked like a small ravine. A puss-like liquid welled up from the wound.

"Look what you've done," Lee said. "You've cut me."

"I've cut you, but there ain't no blood comin' out of the cut I made. How do you explain that?"

Havoc was now convinced that Lee was either a zombie, or something very much like one. He didn't wait for Lee's explanation. Before the chef could answer, he lunged forward with the knife, plunged it into his heart, and pulled it out again. Lee just stood where he was, impassive. Havoc glanced at his knife. There was no blood on the blade. Just something that resembled puss. It was bubbling and hissing.

"What the-?" Havoc said.

He left his question unfinished, because Lee bitch-slapped him on the side of the face. The slap was so hard that it catapulted Havoc sideways onto a catering table, and the knife went flying from his hand. His feet were on the floor but his body was sprawled out over the top of the table, face down.

This was something that had never happened to him before. First, he'd never been caught by surprise like that, and secondly, a slap had never – could never – have knocked him off his feet like that. His head was spinning.

Havoc was vaguely aware of Tyler flying through the air. He shook his head to clear it. He'd been a fool, he told himself. He'd been so surprised by the sight of Lee treating a knife through the heart as if it was a flea bite, that he'd lost his concentration, and now he was paying the price.

There was a clattering of pots and pans as Tyler landed in, or on, something catering-related.

Havoc knew that meant that at any second he could expect Lee to hit him again. Or worse. Just in front of him, on top of the table, there was a cast-iron pan. He reached out and grabbed the handle. His head was clearing a little. He pushed the table top with his hands and stood up quickly, spinning around at the same time, whirling the pan in a vicious arc.

If Lee is behind me, he thought, he's going to get this ol' pan plumb in the chops.

Lee was indeed behind him, his mouth wide open to reveal a set of yellowing and surprisingly sharp-looking teeth. There were strands of gleaming spittle stretching from the top set to the bottom set, and his plan was obviously to take a bite out of Havoc's neck.

The pan put paid to the plan.

It caught Lee exactly where Havoc had intended to catch him, spinning his head round removing a number of teeth into the bargain. Just as lee's head righted itself, Havoc gave him a backhander with the pan that was almost as forceful as the forehand had been. Lee's head spun to the other side, but he didn't fall over, and he didn't look hurt. He looked mad. He reached out and grabbed Havoc's shoulders, his mouth open wide to deliver a fatal bite.

Havoc raised the pan high and rotated his wrists so that the pan was upside down. He rammed it onto the top of Lee's head, so that the crazed chef was wearing it like some sort of a bizarre hat. The pan was so deep that that it completely covered Lee's face Its handle stuck out in front of him, making him look like a child's attempt to portray a Dalek. To add to the effect, the handle moved left and right, as lee shook his head, making it seem as if he was using it as an eye to seek out his enemy.

He tried to remove the pan with both his hands, but the diameter was such that it was stuck fast. Try as he might, he couldn't get it off.

Havoc picked up an American Lodge seasoned cast-iron skillet. It had been made in the legendary 'Steel City' of Pittsburgh, and had been forged by proud American craftsmen who cared about their products. It was the heaviest pan in the kitchen. He tested the balance of it. It felt good.

Havoc held the handle of the skillet in both hands and brought it back, as might a tennis-player who intended to play an unconventional shot: a double-handed forehand, the heaviest shot in the history of tennis. He swung it round in a vicious arc, striking the pan covering Skipper Lee's head with all the force of the clanger striking the bell in the famous Big Ben clock which keeps watch over England's historic parliament buildings on the banks of the river Thames.

BONG!

For all of his fearsome zombie strength, even Skipper Lee struggled to keep his feet. He staggered sideways under the impact.

Havoc smiled. It was an evil little smile, a trademark of his.

The kitchen fell silent as all the staff broke off from their work to look at the source of the noise.

BO-O-O-NG!

This time it was a double-handed backhand, as heavy a shot as any tennis professional has played whilst at the very peak of his career. It was little wonder that under the force of it the chef's knees buckled.

BO-O-O-O-O-NG!!

With this third blow, another forehand, Lee was sent crashing to the floor, where he lay prone and barely moving.

But Havoc was not finished with him yet. Indeed, he had barely begun. He struck the stunned chef on the head another ten times, making a most unlucky total of thirteen, by which point Lee was so dazed and confused that Havoc was able to tie his arms behind his back and truss his legs together with the butcher's string they kept in the kitchen for use when cooking joints of meat.

As Havoc went about his work, he became aware that the sous chefs, dishwashers and other kitchen staff were all staring at him. He raised his head.

"This man is a criminal," he said. "He attacked an officah of the law. Now I'm taking him in."

For a moment he stared back at them. A moment was all it took. They quietly filed away and went back to doing their jobs, as best they could without their boss telling them what to do.

Before long, Havoc had Lee trussed up like a Christmas turkey with the butcher's twine. When he was sure that

Skipper Lee wouldn't be going anywhere, Havoc went over to the corner of the kitchen where Tyler had landed. He was groaning gently.

"I didn't know you were a police officer," he said.

"I'm not, son," Havoc replied. "But don't say that too loudly. Now follow me. You and me, we got us some work to do."

With Havoc's help, Tyler got to his feet.

"What happened?" He asked. "The last thing I remember was seeing you lying on a table as I flew through the air."

"What happened," said Havoc, "is that the zombie feller over there made a big mistake and regretted it. The same mistake a lot of other dead people have made before now."

"What mistake was that?"

"He underestimated Macho Havoc."

I won't ever be making that mistake, Tyler thought to himself.

"Follow me," said Havoc. "We're going to have us a decapitation party."

Havoc led Tyler across the kitchen to the spot where Lee was wriggling like a maggot on the floor. Havoc picked him up and slung him over one shoulder. He left the kitchen with his captive.

"Where are we going?" Tyler asked.

"Somewhere quiet."

Outside they walked along the road to where Havoc had parked his car, a hired Mercedes Coupe. He used his remote to unlock it, opened the boot, and lobbed Lee into it. The burly chef only just fitted in, and Havoc had to press the lid of the boot down with all his weight to get it to shut fully.

"I knew it was a mistake getting this damned little coupe," he said. "I shoulda got a 4 x 4 like I originally planned. Get in, Tyler. We're going for a ride."

Tyler climbed into the passenger side of the vehicle and Havoc drove down the street to a nearby shop which sold electrical supplies. He went in and bought a length of electric cable.

"What did you get that for?" Tyler asked.

"I wanted to get me some rope, but I didn't see no shops selling rope, so I had to get me this instead," Havoc replied.

He took them out of town and pulled up next to a tree which was near the bank of the mighty Potomac River. It was a location which would have made a fine venue for a necktie party in the good old days of the American Wild West.

Havoc took his length of electric flex and tied it around Lee's ankles. He used it to string the chef up from a long branch of the tree about ten feet from the ground. It was a General Cable product, rated to 600 volts, and more than strong enough to bear even the considerable weight of the incapacitated chef, who swung back and forth gently. He spun one way and then the other, on his own axis. Angry noises could be heard from under the pan covering his head. Cuss words, mostly. Then something else: muffled threats.

"You think you've got the better of me don't you? Well, you haven't. Even if you take me out, you won't win. There are too many of us, and we're too well prepared. We're keeping a low profile for now, but when we make our move, you'll all be dead meat. Literally. One of us is going to eat you both. With seasoning."

Havoc rapped the pan on Lee's head with a rock until the chef went quiet.

"I do hope I've got yo' attention Skipper," he said, "because I've got a little surprise for you."

He returned to the car and took a small attaché case from the back seat.

"What's that?" Tyler asked.

"It's my overnight bag. I have all my essential provisions in it."

Havoc opened the case. Tyler shuddered when he saw the contents. It contained a powerful-looking handgun and a sinister knife with a curved blade. Havoc took out the knife.

"I reckon this here knife is sharp enough to cut a man's head clean awf. What do you think, Tyler?"

Tyler nodded. He knew better than to contradict the lethal killing machine known as Macho Havoc. Havoc strode over to the tree. By then, Skipper Lee was wriggling like a maggot on the end of a fishing line.

Havoc took hold of the handle of the pan to steady Lee's head and put the vicious-looking blade of the knife to Lee's throat.

Tyler winced as the blade cut into Lee's flesh.

126

A foul smell erupted from the wound, closely followed by a viscous yellow liquid. Havoc cut through the chef's neck with a sawing action. More puss-coloured liquid came out. It made a hissing noise and fizzed when it met the knife blade.

Havoc stopped cutting and pulled his knife from lee's neck.

"Well, I'll be," he said. He held it up for Tyler to get a good look at it. Much of the blade had been dissolved, as if by a powerful acid.

The blobs of liquid that had fallen from Lee's throat to the ground hissed and bubbled on the bare earth.

"I'm gonna have to try me a different approach," said Havoc.

He had cut a good way through Lee's neck before his knife had become useless. He now took hold of the burly chef's body with one hand to keep it steady, and he took hold of the handle of the pan with the other.

His trademark evil smile played about his lips.

"This here story has a few more twists in it, Tyler," he said.

And he was as good as his word, for he began to turn the pan clockwise by the handle, while holding Lee's body still. He made steady progress, but eventually the pan refused to turn further, and Havoc had to stop and gather up all his strength before continuing. He made a mighty effort, and they heard a noise like the tearing of gristle and the crunching of bone. Then came a veritable Niagara of vile yellow puss from the hapless chef's neck, before, with a crack that resembled the sound of a dry branch being torn from an ancient tree, his head came loose from his body, and Havoc held it triumphantly aloft in the cast-iron pan.

"One thing you forgot to tell me Mistah Tyler," he said, "What's this job payin'?"

Tyler looked embarrassed. He'd been in such a hurry to get Havoc on the job that he hadn't agreed the finer points of the assignment, such as pay, with President Doughnut.

"I'm sorry, Mr. Havoc," he said. "I'm afraid I don't know. The President didn't tell me what he was thinking of paying you for this."

The stone-cold killer's smile of triumph immediately vanished, and was replaced by a menacing glare. He strode up to Tyler and thrust his face close up to that of the smaller man.

"You don't know?" He asked. "YOU DON'T KNOW? You better be joshin' with me boy, 'cause if you ain't, I swear to God I'm gonna-"

He didn't finish his sentence, because at that moment the branch of the tree holding Skipper lee's headless body snapped, and body came crashing to the ground. Both men turned their heads to look at it.

That was when it happened.

Chapter 5

The headless body of the undead chef, with its arms and legs still trussed up, began to wriggle along the ground towards them like some sort of a demented giant worm wriggling with lethal intent through the pages of a Lovecraft-inspired horror story. Tyler looked on in terrified disbelief, transfixed. He was like a rabbit caught in the headlights of a large and very expensive car.

"Well, if that ain't the dangdest thing I ever seen," said Havoc, who was wearing his U.S. Speed Combat Boots with custom-built steel toe-protectors.

He ran over to the writhing thing of evil that the former chef known as Skipper Lee had become, and set about it with his feet, sinking kick after bludgeoning kick into it, booting it first here, and then there, sending it flying this way and that, until at last whatever vile energy was propelling it seemed to depart it for another realm. When it was all over, he wiped his brow with the back of his beefy black hand.

"Whatever yo' boss was thinking of paying me, he better double it," he said. "And then add some mo'. Now let's get outa here."

"But what about him?" Tyler asked.

"Who?"

"Skipper Lee."

"Skipper Lee isn't a him any mo'. He's jest a dead hunk a meat gone off. But you're right. We need to do something. But we can't give him a decent Christian burial, 'cause my suspicion is, he wasn't no Christian. And 'sides, we ain't got no shovels. Tell you what, Tyler, we'll throw him in the Potomac River."

Havoc weighted the body down with stones then he grabbed it by the shoulders.

"You take the feet, Tyler," he said.

Together they carried it to the bank of the Potomac which was only a few yards away.

"All right, get ready now. We're goin' to swing this thing three times then throw it on three. One, two, three!"

The body flew through the air then landed with a splash, quickly disappearing under the waves.

"Now fo' the head," said Havoc.

He picked up the pan containing the severed head of Skipper Lee, pulled back his massive arm, and threw the pan with Lee's head in it as hard as he could. It landed in the middle of the Potomac, where it sank instantly.

And that was the end of Skipper Lee.

Both men climbed into the car. As Havoc put it into 'Drive', Tyler marvelled at his size. The big man looked as though he could barely fit in the space behind the steering wheel of the hired coupe.

"Now, where were we?" Havoc asked, as they set off down the dusty road. "Oh yeah, we were talkin' 'bout money, my least favourite subject. You and yo' boss the President already owe me fo' that Skipper Lee fella. Now we got to sort out the detail of how much you owe me exactly, and what you gonna pay me for the rest of them, and when you gonna pay me."

Tyler nodded.

"I'll have a word with the President," he said.

"The hell you will, Tyler. We're going to pay him a visit together, and I'm gonna talk to him myself, in person."

"But-but-"

"But nuthin'."

Havoc gave Tyler one of his stares and Tyler fell silent for the rest of the journey. Eventually they pulled up at the gates to the White House, and Havoc wound down the windows of the car. Tyler showed the guards his pass.

"Who's that with you, Mr. Tyler?" One of the guards asked.

"Havoc's the name. Macho Havoc."

The two guards looked at each other with expressions of awe on their faces.

"Go straight through, sir," one of them said, opening the gates.

As Havoc drove the car past them, the guards, both of whom were members of America's legendary Marine Corps, snapped to attention and gave him crisp salutes.

Word quickly spread amongst the White House staff that Macho Havoc was visiting the President, so as soon as he pulled up in front of the magnificent front doors, a lackey emerged to park his car for him, and he was waved inside without the slightest of formalities.

"I'll show you to the Oval Office," said Tyler.

"That won't be necessary, son. I know this place like the back of my massive black hand," Havoc replied.

He walked purposefully through the corridors of the building with Tyler trailing in his wake, struggling to keep up with him. When he came to the door of the Oval Office, he opened it and walked through as if it was his right; and in a sense it was, because he had helped more than one American President to get out of a pickle in the course of his illustrious career.

Doughnut was dressed in tennis whites and a visor, striking poses and practising shots with his tennis racquet, like the tennis equivalent of a man playing the air Guitar. His Eastern European girlfriend was sitting at his desk, using the Presidential computer to while away her time on Twitter and Facebook.

When Doughnut saw Havoc, he dropped his tennis racquet in amazement, and his eyeballs traversed up and down Havoc's muscular frame, as did the eyeballs of his girlfriend.

"Who-who are you?" He gasped.

Havoc strode up to him and shook his hand.

"Macho Havoc at your service, Mr. President," he said.

When he heard the name the President's face lit up.

"So you're the guy who's going to get us out of this zombie mess," he said.

"That I am, sir, just as soon as we agree on the rate of pay for the job."

The two men bartered for a few moments, then settled on terms that were acceptable to both, and shook hands on the deal.

Meanwhile Doughnut's girlfriend Natasha had decided there was something about Havoc that she rather liked, which was only to be expected, for he was tall and handsome with a ready grin, and, perhaps because of this, he had a strange power over women. Natasha looked at him as if mesmerised. She left her place at the Presidential desk and walked over to where the two men were standing together.

"Aren't you going to introduce me to your friend?" She asked, in her exotic Eastern European accent.

Glowing with the pride that comes of introducing one esteemed friend to another, Doughnut replied:

"Natasha, meet Macho Havoc, a living legend."

Natasha lowered her eyes coquettishly, and extended her hand. Havoc shook it gently, and felt her press a small folded-up piece of paper into his palm. He surreptitiously slipped it into his pocket.

"Pleased to make your acquaintance, ma'am," he said.

She smiled at him, betraying a strange hunger in the curl of her lips and the cast of her eyes.

"I too am pleased," she said, sashaying back to the Presidential desk to continue her activities on social media.

Havoc wondered what the significance was of the piece of paper she'd given him. He was unable to consider the matter for long, because his thoughts were interrupted by the ringing of his cell phone. He took it from his pocket, looked at it, and grimaced.

"Bad news?" The President asked.

"The worst, sir," said Havoc. "It's a call from my mother."

The President grimaced in sympathy. He had a mother himself, though there were some who doubted he had a father.

"I'll have to take this," Havoc said.

"No need to explain," the President replied.

Havoc put his cell phone to his ear. Everyone in the Oval Office, even Natasha who was several yards away, heard the shrill voice at the other end of the line quite clearly.

"Macho? Is that you?"

"Yes it's me, mother."

"Where you been this past two weeks? I ain't had a single call or visit from you, and I've been worryin' myself sick about you."

"I'll call you back to explain. Right now I'm discussin' important business with the President."

"Never you mind no President. It's me yo' talkin to boy, yo' mother, and you ain't puttin' me off to talk to no President, no matter what yo' business is. You got to get your priorities right, or you'll never amount to anythin'."

Havoc dearly wanted to disconnect her and switch off his mobile phone, but he knew that if he did, she'd do everything in her power to make his life a misery. Not that she didn't seem hell-bent on doing that, anyway.

"There's some folks think I've already done pretty good fo' myself mother. Anyway, I'm all right. How're you keepin'?"

"Are you interested in the answer?"

"I wouldn't have asked if I wasn't interested, would I?" havoc replied, with a distinct sinking feeling in the pit of his stomach.

The President and Tyler both shook their heads.

What followed was an excessively long description of Havoc's mother's ailments, and her problems with her neighbours. With a deal of difficulty, he extricated himself from the conversation.

"Goodbye, Ma. Yeah, yeah, I love you too. G'bye."

He wiped beads of sweat from his brow.

"Well, Mr. President, it seems like my job here is all done, and it's time for me to get on the road and get on with the real job of getting rid of yo' zombie problem."

"Just a minute," said Doughnut. "I've got a report from the C.I.A. for you. You'll need it to carry out your mission. It'll show you where the zombies are located."

"With respect, Mr. President, I wouldn't trust your C.I.A. boys to show me to a fresh turd in a cow-patch. I'll look at your report, but I'll do some huntin' for them myself, if you don't mind."

"Tyler!"

Tyler obediently took the report from the President's desk and handed it to Havoc.

"I'll be going now, Mr President."

"Where are you going exactly?"

"I'll start in Florida, and root out the problem there. Then I'll go to Alabama, Mississippi, and Georgia, and gradually I'll work my way across this whole great continent of ours."

For a moment the President looked troubled.

"Do you really think you can take care of this for me, Havoc?" He asked.

"Leave it to me, sir," Havoc replied, and the two men saluted each other.

Havoc left the building. A flunkey, who had been informed of Havoc's departure, arrived at the front door with Havoc's car as he stepped outside.

"Thank you kindly," Havoc said.

He exchanged salutes with the two marines at the gates then drove to the Watergate Hotel on Virginia Avenue. He checked into his room and took the folded-up piece of paper from his pocket that Natasha had slipped into his hand. There was a telephone number on it with the words *Call me* in distinctly feminine handwriting.

He put the paper to his nose and smelled it. It had a lingering scent of her musky perfume on it.

Havoc poured himself a beer from the mini-bar in and switched on the television. An advert appeared promoting Doughnut and his work as President. He switched channels and saw the very same advert.

"God-dammit," he said.

He took his cell phone from his jacket and rang the number on the piece of paper.

"Hello," said a husky female voice. "Is that Mr. Havoc?"

"It sure is, ma'am, how can I help you?"

"I think you know how you can help me, Mr. Havoc. You can keep me company. Adolf's job takes up so much of his time that I get lonely."

Havoc felt a strange stirring of excitement.

"We all get lonely," he replied. "I'm on my own at the moment, here in room 145 of the Watergate Hotel. I sure could do with some company. When could you come over?"

Back in the White House, Natasha looked at Doughnut's prone form on the bed in their private quarters. He was lying on his back, his gigantic belly rising and falling in time to his snoring. He was taking what he called a 'power nap', which was part of his daily ritual.

"I can come over right now," she said. "I'll meet you in your room."

"All right, looking forward to it."

Natasha wrote out a note quickly, and left it on the bedside cabinet on Doughnut's side of the bed.

'*An old friend asked me to meet her. She's only in Washington for today and tomorrow, and then she flies back to Russia. I'll have to spend some time with her. See you much later xxx*'

She left the room and called Tyler.

"Have my car brought around to the entrance Tyler."

"Right away," he said. "What about your security men?"

"I won't need them."

"Where are you going?"

"That is none of your business. Now get the car."

137

She put a coat of lipstick on her full lips, and checked the effect in the small mirror she kept in her handbag. Satisfied, she left the building, got into her car and drove to the gate. The guards weren't impressed by the fact that she was leaving without any security arrangements, but they knew better than to challenge her about it. Natasha Troubletsky didn't take any shit from anyone, other than very occasionally from her boyfriend the President.

Soon enough, she pulled up outside the Watergate Hotel and despatched a member of the hotel staff to park her car. She entered the foyer, taking a delight in the way that men turned their heads to check her out as she walked by. With her white skin and black hair, her red lips and slim but curvaceous figure, she was as eye-catching as any woman any of them had ever seen. She took the lift to the second floor, found room 145, and tried the door. It was locked. She knocked on it.

"Who's that?"

She immediately recognized Havoc's deep voice.

"It is me, Natasha," she said.

He opened the door and let her in.

"Sorry, ma'am, but you can't be too careful in my line of work."

"Just what is your line of work, Mr. Havoc?"

"Problem solving, Ma'am."

She looked him up and down.

"You can stop calling me ma'am," she said. "Call me Natasha. And I will call you Macho. That is your first name, no?"

Havoc went over to the mini-bar.

"It sure is. Can I fix you a drink?" he asked.

"Vodka, on its own if it is good. If it is no good, give me ice with it."

He held up the bottle for her to see the label.

"Plenty of ice please," she said.

Havoc made the drink and handed it to Natasha. She stood close to him, and he sensed that there was an animal magnetism between them.

"Shall we sit down?" He asked, motioning towards the sofa he had in his room.

"Let us do that," she said.

They both sat on the sofa, which Havoc's frame was almost big enough to fill on its own. Their legs were in close contact. They looked at one another and said nothing. Instead, their faces came slowly, inevitably, closer together, until their lips met. It was the briefest of kisses, and it was followed by a longer one.

"It is very hot in here," said Natasha. "I need to strip off my clothes."

"So do I," Havoc replied.

They went to his bed, and fell upon one another.

Havoc showed Natasha a tenderness that was truly exceptional, and which would never have been returned by his wife, had he been married.

Their lovemaking was mutually satisfying, and lasted for hours, and when at length they stopped, they both felt totally fulfilled.

"You are like a stud stallion, Macho," Natasha breathed in her exotic Russian accent.

"Thank you, Natasha," he replied in his deep southern tones. "You're like a brood mare."

They lay in his bed in each other's arms for a while, moonlight shafting in on them through the windows of Havoc's hotel room, and flashing neon signs illuminating the wall behind them.

"Your brood mare must go now," said Natasha, getting out of the bed.

She dressed rapidly and kissed him on the cheek.

"Text me when you're in town again," she said as she left.

The following morning, Havoc caught a non-stop flight to Miami. He knew that most of the celebrity chef zombies of Florida would be based in Miami. He also knew he would have to act fast, if he was to derail whatever plans they had to take control of his country.

The journey only took two-an-a-half hours, and even allowing for check-in delays and car hire, he was installed in his hotel room by lunch time. He left his hotel without pausing to unpack his bags and walked to the seafront. It was a burning hot day, and all along the beach people were sprawled out sunning themselves, while swimmers were cutting their way through the gentle waves rippling the surface of the otherwise calm sea.

Havoc headed along the coastal road and entered the famous 'Anything Goes' restaurant which overlooked the sea on Miami's South beach. It derived its name from the fact that its owner, Soldier Hawk, was prepared to serve anything, or almost anything, to his customers, including pythons, which he caught himself when hunting in the Everglades.

He was, as his name suggested, a former military man, and an expert in unarmed combat. Havoc was all too aware that Hawk's combat skills allied to his zombie strength would make him a formidable opponent. He decided to follow his usual practice when on a mission of this nature: namely, he would observe his prey, and note any weaknesses, before making his move.

Inside the restaurant, Havoc was grateful for the air-conditioning which gave him respite from the burning Miami heat. He was shown to a table by the maître d'. He ordered a plate of fresh grilled python with seasonal vegetables and hash-browns. When it arrived, he tucked into it with gusto, and while he ate, he kept watch for Soldier Hawk.

It wasn't long before Hawk appeared. Like all good chefs, he went to the trouble of leaving his kitchen on a regular basis to check whether his customers were enjoying his fare. He immediately spotted the powerful African American wolfing down a plate of python, and, intrigued, he went over to Havoc's table.

"Hiya fella, my name's Hawk, and I'm the owner of this here establishment. How're you findin' the python?" He asked.

Havoc put down his knife and fork and dabbed at his lips with a napkin before answering.

"Pleased to meet you, Mr. Hawk," he said. "Your grilled python is as welcome as a steaming hot woman on a sticky night in Alabama."

Hawk grinned and extended his hand, which Havoc shook. He let go and surreptitiously glanced at his fingers. They were covered in concealer.

"Thank you kindly," said Hawk. "If you want anything, just give the waiter a shout, and if he doesn't do the job to your satisfaction, give me a shout."

"I will, Mistah Hawk. Thank you for your personal attention."

Hawk disappeared and Havoc cleared his plate and left, after first visiting the toilets, and examining the security systems protecting the place.

Late that night after the restaurant had closed, Havoc visited it again. He forced entry via the small window to the toilet and made his way into the kitchen. The lights were out and the place was illuminated only by the streetlights and neon lights shining in through the windows.

Havoc hadn't fought in 'Nam, he'd been too young for that. But he'd met plenty of veterans who had, and he'd made a point of finding out everything he could from them about setting traps in the jungle. Here, amidst the jungle of catering equipment, ovens, and hobs, Havoc could see the possibilities of setting a trap for Hawk.

An evil smile played on his lips. He glanced at his watch. He knew that catering staff arrived at their places of work early, and he had only a small amount of time available to set his trap. He intended to use it well.

Before dawn had broken, Havoc had finished con-
structing his man-trap. He congratulated himself on his
efforts. He knew that the veterans who had taught him
his skills would have been proud of the fiendish device
that their pupil had constructed. He moved a few yards
away from the danger area and waited.

Chapter 6

Trapp Fodder rolled over. He hadn't slept at all well. It was a hot night, his house didn't have air-conditioning, and he was covered in sweat. He got out of bed and opened the window.

"What's the matter, honey?" His wife asked.

"Nothin', Martha," he replied. "I'm just so darn hot, that's all. I love Miami, but sometimes the heat gets too darn much for me."

Fodder climbed back into bed. Opening the window hadn't helped, so he resigned himself to being uncomfortable for the rest of the night, and put his head on the pillow. No sooner had he done so than the alarm went off.

Damn!

He'd forgotten he had to get up early today.

He slammed his hand on the clock to shut it up and got out of bed again.

"What time is it?" Martha Fodder asked.

"Never mind, just get back to sleep," he replied. "I've got to go to work early today, I told you about it last night, remember?" He said.

He showered, dressed, and drove through the darkness to his place of work. The city streets were quiet at this time in the morning. He parked in the small staff car park – one of the few perks of his job – and unlocked the back door. He hung up his jacket in the narrow corridor that lay just beyond the door, and made his way to the end of it and opened a second door. He stepped through the doorway, reached to one side of it, and snapped the light switch to the 'on' position.

As the overhead lights flickered into life, he felt a series of ropes whip around his body, lashing his arms to his sides. Almost in the same moment, he was hoisted into the air. He cried out in alarm, but there was no-one to hear him, and, in any event, there was not a man or woman on the planet who could have done anything to stop what happened next.

A long wooden pole on a powerful spring swept sideways with a vicious scything action. At the end of the pole there was a long-bladed kitchen knife that was as sharp as any knife that had ever been made. This knife struck Fodder on the lower part of his forehead just above the eyebrows, slicing off the top of his head, as would a sous-chef slice off the end of a soft-boiled egg with a knife. The top of Fodder's skull flew like a flying saucer through the air and fell on a worktop several yards distant. The noise it made as it clattered along the stainless-steel surface was music to Havoc's ears.

A second wooden pole swooped down – this one had a saucepan tied to the end of it – and it scooped out Fodder's brain as would a man scoop out the yolk of his breakfast egg with a spoon, and deposited it on the immaculately polished kitchen floor with a soggy plop.

Havoc, who had been watching the whole thing from a place of concealment behind a piece of kitchen apparatus, came out of his hiding place and looked up at the corpse of Fodder, which was swinging gently at the end of a rope above his head.

"Well I'll be," he muttered. "You ain't Soldier Hawk. Just who in tarnation are you?"

At that moment, the back door opened and slammed shut, so Havoc dropped into a crouch behind another large item of kitchen apparatus.

In walked Soldier Hawk, who stopped dead when he saw the corpse of his loyal manager Trapp Fodder swinging gently in the air above him, bits of goo still spilling from the rim of his skull and dripping to the floor with a plop-plop-plop sound.

Hawk looked left and right, sniffed the air, then bent down, picked up Fodder's brain, sniffed it, bit off a piece and began chewing the rubbery tissue. Rivulets of blood ran from the corners of his mouth, staining his immaculate white chef's outfit.

"Mmmmm," he said, appreciatively. "Fresh and still warm. I'll put this in the fridge and cook it later today. I know you're here, by the way, whoever you are. I can smell you. You had a meal in my restaurant the other day. I'm coming to get you as soon as I've dealt with this fine succulent brain."

Havoc watched as Hawk put the brain on a plate and wrapped it carefully in Clingfilm. When he'd finished, Hawk opened a padlocked fridge. It was full of body parts.

He put the brain inside, shut the fridge door and closed the padlock.

"Whoever you are, stranger, you'll be joining my manager's brain in that fridge soon," he said, and then he began sniffing the air like a dog. He followed his nose, which took him in the direction of Havoc's hiding place.

Havoc stood up. There was no point in hiding any longer. He reached into his jacket and pulled his gun from its holster, intending to blow Hawk's brains out with it. But Hawk, being a fighter himself, launched forward and slapped the gun from havoc's hand before it was levelled at his head. Havoc snapped out his jab, taking care to avoid the slavering jaws of the zombie chef, and rocked back the chef's head.

The door opened and another member of Hawk's staff entered the kitchen.

Boulder Todd.

Havoc knew he couldn't afford to try to fight two opponents at once, so he ran towards Todd, intending to take him out, and then turn his attentions back to Hawk.

Boulder Todd was a big man, bigger even than Havoc, standing six feet six inches tall and weighing in at a colossal two hundred and fifty pounds, all of it muscle.

Todd was a skilled fighter, having taken up boxing at an early age, and won the super-heavyweight division of the American Golden Gloves championship no fewer than five times while he was still in his teens. He was known as 'Boulder' because his pink shaven head was unusually hard and spherical, and could absorb the weightiest of blows without its owner ever showing even the slightest signs of discomfort. He had never been knocked off his feet, far less knocked out, either inside the boxing ring, or on the cruel streets of Philadelphia where he had grown up and honed his skills.

He knew all there was to know about fist-fighting, and it was this knowledge that he now intended to put to concussive effect on Havoc.

He advanced, bobbing and weaving to present a difficult target, his right fist cocked to deliver the knockout blow, his left feinting and probing for openings in Havoc's defence.

The blow that felled Boulder Todd seemed to come from nowhere. It hit him plumb in the middle of the forehead and deposited him flat on his back several yards away. He was unconscious before he hit the deck, before, indeed, his massive feet had even left the ground.

It was Havoc's trademark punch that had done for him, which he called his "Bull-hammer", and fortunate indeed was the bull that could say it had crossed his path and not been knocked senseless by it at one time or another.

Having disposed of Todd, Havoc turned to confront Hawk, who was now advancing on him, neck-jutting and clacking his teeth like a pair of deadly castanets. Havoc tried out his Bull-Hammer, but this did no more than rock the chef's head back for a moment. He looked around for a weapon, a kitchen knife, or even a spoon, anything to strike the chef with, but there was nothing within reach. Then his eyes fell on a knife rack a few yards away and he ran towards it. Before he'd gone more than two paces his foot landed in a pool of slippery matter that had been discharged from the open skull of Trapp Fodder the under-manager, who was still watching proceedings from above, albeit with oddly dull-looking eyes.

Havoc's foot immediately skidded out from beneath him and he fell painfully to the floor. Hawk, sensing his opportunity, dived through the air, arms close by his sides, jaws agape, intending to land on Havoc and deliver a killer bite.

Havoc rolled to one side just in time, and Hawk's teeth smashed harmlessly into the kitchen floor. Havoc delivered a karate chop to the back of hawk's neck while the chef was face down, but it had no effect, and the chef raised his head, looked at Havoc and waved his finger in admonishment.

They both jumped to their feet and Hawk fastened his hands around Havoc's neck. Havoc tried a knee to the balls, but it made no difference. The pressure on his throat increased. The chef brought his face closer to Havoc's, mouth open, teeth bared. Havoc tried to push him away, but even his immense strength wasn't sufficient to overcome that of the zombie chef. He knew that if he didn't do something quickly – very quickly – his larynx would be crushed, and that would be the least of his problems.

He held onto the chef's lapel with one hand, and with the other he made a two-fingered strike deep into both of Hawk's eyes. Havoc had long, strong, fingers, which penetrated several inches into the chef's eye sockets with a meaty squelch, plunging deep into the frontal lobes of his brain.

"Aaaargh!" Cried Hawk.

He let go of Havoc and staggered backwards, blobs of jelly and puss-like liquids oozing from the dark sockets that had only moments ago been the home for his eyes. Havoc felt a burning sensation on his fingers and immediately wiped them clean of the foul stuff that had soiled them. In the second or two it took him to wipe them clean, the chef rallied himself.

Maddened with pain, he roared and charged blindly forward.

Havoc stepped to one side like a matador and the chef crashed into a worktop with such force that he ended up bent double over the top of it. Havoc picked up a cleaver, and, as the chef got himself upright and turned around, Havoc sank the cleaver into his skull and let go of the handle.

With the cleaver stuck deep into his scalp, and his two eyeless orbits oozing fluids, the chef's head now looked like nothing so much as a particularly horrifying Halloween mask.

He staggered around the kitchen flailing his arms, crashing into one item after another, sending pots and pans, and kitchen utensils, flying everywhere, then at length he fell to the floor, where he twitched feebly for a few minutes, before ceasing to move altogether. Above him, Fodder looked on with a doleful expression on what was left of his face, as if saddened by his master's demise.

Havoc looked around the kitchen.

"This is a whole lotta mess to clear up," he said to himself. "Well, I suppose I best get started."

He moved the bodies to a back store-room and locked it, mopped and cleaned the floor, and removed all trace of his man-trap.

He'd gotten rid of the zombie chef, but he knew from what he'd seen that the kitchen staff had been somehow enslaved by the chef, and he feared they'd remain loyal to the zombie cause, and support the other zombies in their efforts to take over his beloved country. He wondered what he should do. Then the answer came to him. An evil smile played on his lips.

Later that day, the restaurant had to function without the benefit of its owner Hawk, or its under-manager Fodder, or Boulder Todd, who'd been a key member of staff. But function it did, as the workforce was well-trained.

By the early afternoon it was in full-swing, with the chefs rushing around making meals by the dozen. Then one of them made the mistake of switching on a hob that Havoc had tinkered with.

Chapter 7

KA-BOOM!

Chapter 8

The issues with humans supporting the zombie takeover were ended in an instant. At least, the problem of those supporters who worked at 'Anything Goes' was.

Unfortunately, there was a degree of collateral damage, as the restaurant was full of diners, who, until their meals had been interrupted by the explosion, had been enjoying themselves.

There were any number of shoppers who had their day ruined as well, because the rows of shops to either side of 'Anything Goes' were flattened by the blast.

Havoc was saddened by what he saw, as he watched from a beach bar at a safe distance from the effects of the explosion (although a small amount of debris from the blast rained on it for several seconds). But, being a soldier, he knew that you couldn't make an omelette without breaking eggs, and he resolved to take the best possible care of the eggs in future, while still endeavouring to make the very finest of omelettes.

He got out of his chair in the shade and walked a couple of hundred yards along the South Beach seafront to the next restaurant which was called Sloppy Sam's. Sam insisted on drizzling his specialty sauces over every dish he made, hence the name. Havoc ordered a plate of rib-eye steaks done rare, with Sam's chilli pepper sauce drizzled over them, and a side dish of eggs over-easy with Sam's special egg sauce.

Blowing up stuff and killing folk can make a man like me mighty hungry, he said to himself, as he guzzled down his meal with gusto. Every now and then he raised his head and looked around the restaurant, in the hope of seeing Sloppy Sam.

He was very much looking forward to terminating the zombie career of his next celebrity chef victim.

Chapter 9

A few days later President Doughnut was sitting at his desk scanning through the latest report from the C.I.A. When he'd digested the contents, or as much of them as he cared to take in, he got on the White House internal phone system.

"Tyler, get over here right now!" He barked.

Then he put the receiver forcibly back onto the cradle, stood up, and paced around. He was wearing swimming shorts and a bathrobe in preparation for his dip later that morning.

After a minute or two there was a knock on the door of the Oval Office.

"Come in!"

Tyler walked through the door and shut it behind him.

The President had his back to Tyler and was looking out of the window at the rolling lawns outside. His hands, which were clasped behind his back, were clutching a sheaf of papers of some kind. He turned around and pointed the papers at Tyler.

"What's the meaning of this?" He demanded.

Tyler saw that the President's face was red and blotchy.

"The meaning of what, Mr. President?"

"The deaths from the war we're waging. We're taking heavy casualties. Tremendously heavy casualties."

"What war? Do you mean the war with the zombies? Are the zombies killing a lot of our people?"

"No, you damned fool. Our own one-man army is killing a lot of our people. Havoc is costing us more lives than all the zombies put together. He was meant to be running a low-profile operation. We can't afford to win the war this way, or I'll be sunk at the next election. We need to find another way of getting rid of the zombies, a way that won't result in so many deaths, and won't alarm the American voters. Who else do we know besides Havoc who's an expert on killing them?"

"The British Prime Minister. He's the one who can help us. He cleared the zombies out of his own country a few months ago. He's called Camemblert. You've met him a couple of times, remember?"

"Camemblert? That ass-hole? You've got to be fucking kidding me. He can't fart and chew gum at the same time."

"Well, he does seem to have gotten rid of the zombies they had over in England, sir."

"I can't go to that stuck-up ass-hole Camemblert for advice. I'd sooner see the U.S. of A. overrun by zombie commies than do that."

"That's what it might come to, sir, if you don't ask him how he did it."

Tyler picked up the receiver and dialled Camemblert's number. He immediately got through to the switchboard at 10 Downing Street.

"Yes, how can I help?" It was a female voice speaking in immaculate upper-class brit tones.

Tyler felt himself go weak at the knees. Like all Americans, he was a sucker for a posh British accent.

"It's the American President on the line for Prime Minister Camemblert," he said.

"Putting you through now sir," she replied.

Tyler held the receiver out to Doughnut.

"You're being put through even as we speak, sir," he said, covering the mouthpiece of the receiver with his hand. "You better speak to him nicely."

"All right then, I'll do my best," Doughnut growled. "But that limey ass-hole better not push me too far this time. I've had just about as much as I can take from that patronising bastard. What's he called again?"

"Camemblert, pronounced like the cheese. His first name is Tarquin."

"Tarquin, what kind of a name is that?"

Reluctantly, Doughnut took the receiver from his aide and put it to his ear. There was a male voice with a stuck-up limey accent on the line.

"Camemblert here."

Doughnut twitched his toothbrush moustache in annoyance.

"Tarquin, it's me, Adolf, the American President."

"Adolf, how nice to hear from you. How are things over in Washington D.C.?"

"Couldn't be better Tarquin. How are things in Limey-land, I mean, England?"

"Thoroughly spiffing. We had a few sticky moments a couple of months ago with some zombies. I got my Foreign Secretary to ring and tell you about that, do you re-member?"

"Yeah, kind of."

"Anyway, I had this brainwave about how to deal with the zombies and we completely got rid of them. Problem solved. How are you getting on with them on your side of the pond?"

"That's what I'm calling about. We're plugging away, you know, getting on top of the situation, and we defi-nitely have it under control, but if you have a few tips you can share with me, well, you know me, Tarquin, I'm always keen to listen to advice."

Camemblert, who was slouching at his desk, pushed his chair, which was on castors, backwards, and put his feet up on the desk with his legs crossed. He leaned further back in his chair.

"Advice," he said. "We British are always keen to help our American friends with advice when we can. You know how much we value our special relationship with you, Adolf," he said.

Doughnut felt his blood pressure rising. He breathed deeply.

"We value it too. Now about that advice-"

"Tell you what," said Camemblert, "why don't you come over, and we'll have a chat about it. We could call it a summit meeting. We wouldn't have to tell the public what it was all about. I never tell them anything, anyway, not when I can help it. What do you say?"

"I'm a bit pushed for time, Tarquin. Why don't you just give me your advice over the phone?"

Camemblert yawned and stretched out his free arm.

"I'm sorry, I can't do that. I'm on my way to an important meeting. Look, you get your people to talk to my people and arrange a date to come over and we'll talk about it then, okay?"

Limey asshole, thought Doughnut.

"That'd be wonderful, Tarquin. I'm looking forward to it."

"So am I. See you soon."

"Yeah, see yah soon."

Part III: England Again

Chapter 1

The boyishly handsome Prime Minister put down his telephone and sighed.

"Do you know something, Johnson?" He said, moving a cowlick of his black hair from his eyes with his hand. "That's the sixth this morning, and it's not even ten o'clock."

"The sixth what, Prime Minister?" Asked Johnson, his aide, as he decanted the teacups from the tray he'd just brought into the P.M.'s office at number ten Downing Street.

"The sixth Head of State, Johnson. Haven't you been listening to a word I've been saying?"

"Of course I've been listening, Prime Minister," said Johnson. "I wouldn't want to miss a single one of your pearls of wisdom, now, would I?"

The P.M. scrutinised Johnson's face carefully for signs of sarcasm, but not a single muscle on it flickered.

"Nor do the Heads of State it seems," he said, after an awkward pause. "They're all asking me for advice."

"I'm sure you're more than capable of giving it to them, Prime Minister," Johnson muttered urbanely as he stirred the tea.

"I ought to be by now," said the P.M. "I've told any number of them how to go about getting rid of their problem."

"That would be the zombie problem, I presume, Prime Minister."

"That's right, Johnson. That was Doughnut, the American President, on the line. One month ago, people like him wouldn't have given me the time of day. Now, just because I've single-handedly got rid of the plague of zombies from this fine country of ours, they're queueing up to talk to me to find out how I did it, even that stroppy Russian leader, whatsisname, Putrid. He was on the blower first thing this morning asking me what to do about his zombies. This could be the dawning of a new age for our country. We could become world leaders once again. I could be the man who puts the great back into Great Britain." He jutted out his jaw in his characteristic determined way. "We feel the hand of fate on our shoulder," he said.

Johnson raised an eyebrow.

"*We*, sir?"

The P.M ignored him.

"Some of them have been laughing at us behind our backs for years," he continued. "Now they're going to get their come-uppance. We're going to be laughing behind their backs from now on, because they're going to have to listen to us for a change, especially the yanks. The yanks have been getting right up my wick for long enough. Now it's my turn to get right up their wicks. I'm going to tell them to stop bossing us around and finally admit that the British way of doing things is best, and always has been the best."

"Very good, Prime Minister," said Johnson, placing a teacup on a pile of papers in front of the P.M. Most of the papers had circular brown stains on them.

"Have you looked at the opinion polls this morning Johnson?" The P.M. asked.

"Not yet, Prime Minister."

"Make it your next job. You need to know how popular I am."

"I already have a very good idea of how popular you are in most quarters, Prime Minister."

The P.M. looked hard at Johnson, who maintained his usual deadpan expression.

"Be that as it may, you need to keep abreast of how popular I am with the Great British Public. They're the ones who vote for me, after all. I've already checked. I've been checking every day this week, as a matter of fact. Do you know I've got the highest ratings of any Prime Minister in history?"

"Indeed, Prime Minister."

"Do you know why, Johnson?"

"I can't say I do, Prime Minister."

"It's because I'm presiding over a grateful nation, that's why."

Johnson raised an eyebrow.

"Presiding? I thought we were a monarchy."

"All right, ruling then."

"Ruling?"

"You know full well what I mean, Johnson. Prime Min-istering, or whatever it is that I do. Anyway, my nation is grateful because I'm making such a bloody good job of it. I was going to give it up, but I've decided it would be very selfish of me to deprive the nation of the benefit of having me as Prime Minister, when they clearly want me to go on, so I'm going to call a snap election in a few weeks before they change their minds. You know how fickle the public can be."

"That's wonderful news, Prime Minister," said Johnson, in a tone of voice that didn't quite live up to the enthusiasm of his words.

"Anyway, that's why it's important for you to check how popular I am. I'll be too busy campaigning from now on to look at the opinion polls every day, and I want you to do it for me. I want you to keep me up to date on how popular I am, because if my ratings slip, I might have to call the election off until they improve again."

"I see."

"By the way Johnson, I've thought of a fantastic wheeze to keep my face in the news and boost my ratings even higher."

"What might that be Prime Minister?"

"I'm going to declare a national holiday."

"What's this new-fangled holiday of yours going to be all about?"

"I'm going to call it V.O.Z. day, short for 'Victory over Zombies Day', and it's going to commemorate Great Britain winning the war against the zombies. It'll be a bit like a combination of Bonfire Night and V.E. day. My people can let off fireworks and have street parties, and that kind of thing. We'll encourage them to dress up as zombies. That should get everyone onside, or almost everyone, including even some of the plebs who'd never normally vote for me in a month of Sundays."

"But perhaps not the plebs of Huddersfield, Prime Minister," said Johnson, taking a sip of his tea.

The P.M. reddened.

"It's not my fault that I had to bomb Huddersfield because it was full of zombies, Johnson," he said. "Anyway, we can make it up to them. What do they do up there in Huddersfield? Clog-dancing, isn't it? That's what I've heard. Well, we can have clog-dancing at the street parties to show our support for Huddersfield. In fact, we can do more than that. We can have zombie-themed parties with the dancers dressed up as zombies. Just think of it. Clog-dancing zombies honouring the sacrifices made by the plucky town of Huddersfield. That should shut those stroppy northerners up."

He took a languid sip of his tea.

"Where was I? Oh yes, the V.O.Z. day celebrations. President Doughnut is visiting me to get advice about how to deal with his zombie problem. I'll schedule his visit to coincide with V.O.Z. day so he'll be able to see for himself that the British people know how to get shot of zombies, and have a bloody good knees-up afterwards. That'll get right up his wick, I tell you."

"That will be absolutely splendid, Prime Minister."

The P.M. took another sip of his tea.

"Order some bunting in, will you, Johnson, we'll need to decorate the State Room for when the President comes over to celebrate V.O.Z. day with us. You might as well order some zombie outfits and clogs while you're at it, so we can lay on some themed entertainment for him."

"Very good, Prime Minister."

"Oh, another thing. Have you heard any news about Bertie?"

"Bertie who, Prime Minister?"

"Bertie Doodah, the Queen's tenth cousin twice removed. He went to President Doughnut's topping-out ceremony for that preposterous wall of his, and he hasn't been seen since. He probably got lost and couldn't find his way home. He isn't the sharpest tool in the box. None of these royals are. That's why they're so good at their job. They don't think deeply about anything; they just get on with it. Sometimes I wish I was like them."

"Perhaps you are, Prime Minister."

"What was that?"

"Nothing, Prime Minister. Bertie was killed along with your Foreign Secretary when a plane crashed onto the wall. Have you already forgotten about that?"

"If I have, it's understandable. I have a lot on my mind. It's not all beer and skittles running this great country of ours, you know. Now instead of having a go at me, why don't you concentrate on getting the bunting for the Presidential knees-up?"

"Very well, prime Minister."

Chapter 2

Doughnut slammed down the receiver of his telephone in the Oval Office, his face flushed with anger.

"Who does that God-damned limey ass-hole think he is?" he fumed. "He thinks he can talk to me how the hell he likes, just because he's got rid of a few zombies from that worthless little strip of dirt he lives on. What's it called again?"

The President's aide looked up from his iPhone.

"Even the limeys themselves aren't sure what it's called, sir," he said. "They sometimes call it the United Kingdom, or the U.K. for short. The U.K. comprises of four countries: England, Scotland, Wales and Northern Ireland."

The President's eyes began to glaze over. His aide continued regardless.

"They have a few other names for it, too. Great Britain is one of them. Strictly speaking, that refers to the island off the coast of Western Europe in the -"

The president cut him short.

"I don't care what the hell it's called," he said. "That limey sonofabitch thinks he can get one over on me. The reason he wants me to go over there is so that he can show off to the rest of the limeys that I'm at his beck and call. Well, I'll show him. Make sure we take the biggest motorcade over there that any American President ever took to any country. I want to make him look like the poor relation, and I want it to be clear to everyone watching on television that he *is* the poor relation.

And another thing. Just in case he tries anything underhand, get the White House PR team at the ready. We need to put the right spin on this, and kill any stories about it that might be negative to us. Is that clear, Tyler?"

"Yes, Mr President. I'll get right on it."

Chapter 3

Prime Minister Camemblert adopted a thoughtful frown. He held it for exactly five seconds and did a little chin rubbing while he was at it for good measure. Then he thrust his jaw forward and gave his visitors one of his best-ever determined Churchillian looks.

"Leave it with me, gentlemen," he said. "I won't let you down."

The burghers of Huddersfield, who were all Tories, had come to him with their caps in their hands seeking funds to rebuild their town. They felt reassured by this.

Prime Minister Camemblert had ordered the bombing of Huddersfield to cleanse it of zombies; and they knew from the Churchillian look he was giving them that they could rely on him to secure funds for them to repair the damage it had caused.

"Thank you Prime Minister," they chorused, with much tugging of forelocks. "Thank you ever so much."

As if hypnotised, they all stood up and allowed themselves to be ushered by the PM out the door of Number 10, without any promise of any money whatsoever. He waved them goodbye from the door, a cheery smile on his face for the benefit of the waiting press, as flashbulbs popped all around him.

He was vaguely aware of the burghers giving interviews to the press as they made their way down Downing Street.

"I won't let you down," he heard them saying, as they quoted his words to the press.

He finished waving and allowed himself the luxury of a satisfied smile, as he shut the front door of Number 10. They were quoting his very words! That would be great for his image.

He went back to his office, and then he had a terrifying thought. What was he going to do, to avoid letting them down? He had no idea.

He picked up the telephone and called his aide.

"Johnson," he said. "Get in here at once. I need you for a brainstorming session."

A few minutes later, Johnson entered the P.M.'s office with his 'House of Commons' ballpoint pen and pad, the ones with the portcullis logo on them. He sat down opposite the P.M.

"What are we brainstorming about, Prime Minister?" He asked.

"Huddersfield," said Camemblert. "The town's burghers came here asking for money, and I sent them packing saying I wouldn't let them down, but I can't give them any money, the Chancellor wouldn't stand for it. And besides, it's against my tory principles. So, I need to think of some other way to make them happy; or at least, to not get any bad publicity out of it."

"Quite, Prime Minister. Who's going to start with the brainstorming session? You or me?"

"I don't know. Yes, I do. Me. No, you."

"How about asking the Chancellor for money from his contingency budget?"

"I've just told you, the Chancellor won't stand for it."

"Well, there's nothing to be lost by asking him."

"Yes there is, I don't like him and I don't like spending time with him. Have you ever seen those looks he gives me? I'd sack him right now if it wasn't for the fact that his supporters would use it as an excuse to get rid of me."

"We seem to have an impossible problem then, Prime Minister."

"Nothing is impossible, Johnson. Look at me. I'm Prime Minister and people said that was impossible."

"They're still saying it," Johnson muttered.

"What was that?"

"Nothing, Prime Minister."

"Wait a minute, I've got it. I've got the answer. Trickle-down."

"What's trickle-down?"

"It's where rich people spend money somewhere, and the poor people benefit as a result."

"You mean like living off the scraps that fall off the table?"

"A bit like that, yes. No, no. What are you saying Johnson? It's a way of helping people to help themselves, rather than creating a nation of scroungers. Now let me think. How can we get people to spend money in a place like Huddersfield?"

"How indeed Prime Minister? There are no shops there any more to spend money in. You bombed them all flat, remember?"

"We can set up market stalls then. Or the people of Huddersfield can set them up. Wait, it's just come to me, I know exactly what we should do. We've got an approved budget for entertaining the American President while he's over here. We can use the money to pay for the V.O.Z day celebrations that take place in Huddersfield, and we can take the president there. We'll send our best troupes of clog-dancing zombies up to Huddersfield to impress him. That way, we can revive the fortunes of the ailing little town without actually spending any money on it, as such. I bet you the townsfolk will make a mint on V.O.Z day just by setting up a decent tombola stand in St George's Square."

"A tombola stand? - Brilliant, Prime Minister. That's just what's needed to revive the flagging fortunes of a once-proud woollen town in the north of England."

"Well, you better get to it Johnson."

"Get to what, Prime Minister?"

"Telling the people of Huddersfield about their good fortune."

"What good fortune would that be, Prime Minister?"

"That instead of simply taking the easy way out, and giving them a pile of cash to rebuild their town with, we're dealing with their problem in an imaginative way. We're trickling down funds to them from the private sector, and we're using V.O.Z day to do it."

"Oh I see. *That* good fortune Prime Minister. I rather thought you'd want to tell them about that yourself, as it was your idea."

"I would, Johnson, but I'm busy preparing for P.M.Q.'s, and anyway, I know how you like to hob-nob with the press whenever we've got a good story to tell, so I'm putting it in your capable hands."

"I will be eternally grateful to you for that, Prime Minister."

Chapter 4

The news of the many deaths in the sleepy Yorkshire village of Nobblethwaite was reported nationally.

A spook, intrigued by the news, hacked into the police computers at the Nab Police H.Q., and read the reports of eight deaths, all of them seemingly caused by a wild animal, which some witnesses described as a domestic cat, and others as a tiger. There was even a suggestion that it was a were-cat.

The forensic analysis of the corpses was baffling. It confirmed that the creature that was responsible was indeed a cat. But no domestic cat could have wreaked such havoc.

Unless, of course, it was another zombie cat like the one that had been on the rampage in London and Huddersfield during the recent war with the zombies.

The spook compiled a report and sent it to the head of MI5, and the head of MI5 sent it to Johnson, the P.M.'s aide. Johnson decided he should bring it to the attention of the P.M. immediately.

The P.M. was burdened with paperwork as usual.

And as usual, he couldn't be bothered with it. He left it lying on his desk amongst the ever-growing piles and read the morning papers instead. He found that far more enjoyable than any of the official documents he was supposed to read.

When Johnson brought the report from MI5 into his office at Number 10 Downing Street, the P.M. looked up from the Daily Mail.

"What's that you've got Johnson?" He asked. "It's not another bloody report, is it? Because if it is, I'm sick to the back teeth of them. Just put it there, will you?"

He waved his arm airily over the many piles of papers, some of them as much as two-foot-high that were stacked up on his desk.

Johnson didn't move.

"What are you waiting for?" The P.M. asked.

He pointed at the biggest pile of papers, which had a patina of dust on top it. "Put it there, man. I'll get around to it."

Johnson ignored these instructions and thrust the report towards the P.M.

"There's no time to lose, Prime Minister. You have to read this right now," he said.

"Oh, do I? You listen to me Johnson, you can't tell me what to do. I'm the top banana around here, and I can do what the bloody hell I like."

"Of course you can, Prime Minister. However, I feel I should draw your attention to the fact that there appears to be a zombie cat, or zomcat as MI5 are calling them, running around in Nobblethwaite, a village in West Yorkshire not too far removed from Huddersfield. One can only speculate about how silly you'd look if news were to break about an undead cat running riot during the President's visit, given that you've told him that you've wiped out all the zombies. And what if he were to see the thing for himself? Heaven forbid that that should happen."

The P.M. lowered his newspaper and thrust his jaw forward.

"You're right, Johnson. We can't allow that. We've got to get rid of the thing. But we don't want Johnny Public to know about it, not after we've told him we've got rid of all the zombies. We need to sort it out on the Q.T. Let me see. What can we do?"

"Send in a small group of the S.A.S., Prime Minister."

The P.M. sighed petulantly.

"If we did that, everybody would know we had a problem, Johnson. I know, let's get that chap onto it."

"What chap?"

"The one we used last time. You know, Ensign Pennant or whatever he's called."

"You mean Flagg Banner, Prime Minister."

"That's right. It's a bloody silly name, if you ask me. That's why I couldn't remember it."

"A bit like Camemblert, then."

"What? What's that, Johnson?"

"Nothing, I'll get in touch with Mr. Banner right away. Will that be all, Prime Minister?"

"Yes, that will be all for now, Johnson."

Chapter 5

He sat at his kitchen table perusing the dossier that he'd been given by his MI5 handler. It gave him precious little to go on.

In summary: there was a village called Nobblethwaite, any number of witnesses who'd seen things that didn't add up, not even with each other, let alone with any possible underlying reality, and there were no pictures.

But he'd seen enough in his time to know that, even so, it might mean there was a threat to his country that had to be exterminated – and he prided himself on his ability to exterminate threats.

He stood six feet one-inch-tall, was lantern-jawed, and had a wiry strength that belied his slim physique. His name was Flagg Banner, and it was a name that was feared throughout the British Isles.

Banner unfurled himself from his chair, moved with an easy grace to the kitchen and made a mug of tea. With his mug of tea in his hand, he gave some thought to the tools he'd need for his latest job. When he'd finished his tea, he packed a specially adapted suitcase with the tools he'd chosen. He put some clothes in an overnight bag, and threw the suitcase and bag into the back of his car, a green Land Rover Defender that looked as though it would be at home on a battlefield.

He climbed into the car and drove north up the M1, turning off the motorway at junction 24 to drive to Nobblethwaite. Due to the many road works on the M1 the journey took up the entire day and most of the evening, so it was 10.30 p.m. by the time he reached his destination. He pulled up in the car park of the Ne'er Do Well inn, took his bags from his car, and walked through the front door.

For a village pub, it was surprisingly busy. Banner heard a hubbub of conversation as soon as he stepped inside. Within seconds of his entry, it stopped and heads turned to look at him. He narrowed his eyes and returned the stares. No-one held his gaze. Satisfied that he'd laid down a marker, he went to the bar and looked at the names of the beers on offer. Behind him, the hubbub of conversation resumed.

"I'll have a pint of Nobblethwaite Best, please," he said, "and a room for the night."

The landlady surreptitiously looked him up and down to get the measure of him, as she did with all the strangers who visited her pub, and then she got a glass and pulled the stranger a pint.

"You don't sound like you come from these parts," she said.

"I'm not, I'm from London."

The landlady nodded. She'd suspected him of being a southerner. She took a set of keys from the wall behind her and held them towards him.

"See that door?" She asked, indicating a door at the back of the room.

Banner nodded.

"There's some stairs at the back of it. Your room's the first on the right at the top."

Banner held out his hand to take the keys from her. She pulled her own hand back.

"Not so fast," she said. "We don't want any trouble around here. We won't stand for it. Have you got that?"

Banner's lips curled into a smile.

"I've got it," he said. "Now kindly give me the keys."

Against her better judgement, the landlady handed them over.

He looked around the room for someone to talk to who looked as if he might be a promising source of information. His eyes soon settled on a group of three old men sitting at a table in the corner. He picked up his two bags with one hand as if they weighed nothing, and with his pint in the other, he went over to their table and put his pint on it. Once again, the hubbub of conversation stopped and all the eyes in the crowded pub fell on him.

"Mind if I join you?" He asked.

Without waiting for an answer, he placed his bags on the floor and pulled up a chair.

"Cheers," he said, taking a sip of his drink.

"You don't want to linger in these parts," said one of the old men.

"Why not?"

The old man shook his head.

"T' curse of t'Slawits," he said.

"The curse of what?"

The old man took a long pull of an e-cigarette; the end glowed bright red.

"T' curse of t'Slawits. They were a family that used to live up on the big hill outside the village. Nodger Hill we call it. T'Slawits had a gipsy curse put on 'em nearly three hundred years ago. They used to own all the land round here as far as he eye can see, including this village. The last of 'em still owns a lot of it. But it's all cursed, and so are we. So, you'd best not stay too long, or you'll end up cursed too."

"This curse, what does it do to you?"

"It's not what it does to us; it's what it does to t'Slawits."

"Tell me more."

"It's turned 'em into a family of were-cats."

"Were-cats? What are they?"

"They're like were-wolves but worse. They're men that change into cats, big buggers they are, like lions or tigers, and they'll tear you to pieces as soon as look at yer."

Another of the old men took an e-pipe from his mouth and pointed the stem at Banner.

"Don't take any notice of Sam," he said. "He doesn't know what he's talking about. There's no curse and no were-cats. There's some'at afoot, though, that's for sure."

Banner narrowed his eyes.

"What do you reckon it is, then?" He asked. "If it's not a were-cat?"

"You'll have heard of the Beast of Bodmin Moor. We've got one of them up here. Let's call it the Beast of Nobble Moor. It's a big bugger just like Sam says, and it's vicious, too. It killed five men 'ere last week, right outside this pub, and it'll have you too, if you don't watch yer step, so think on."

"Bloody 'ell," said the third of the trio. "I've never heard anything so daft in all me puff as what these two have just been telling thee. You know these rich folk as don't 'ave anything better to do than keep exotic animals? I reckon one of 'em down in Huddersfield or Barnsley had a big cat like a cougar or some'at like that, and it escaped. Naturally, the owner couldn't let on, because what he was doing was illegal. Anyway, that cougar or whatever it is, it's living on Nobble Moor, and it's been surviving by eating deer and rabbit. But it's got a taste for human blood now, and you mark my words, it'll be back 'ere, and when it is, there'll be hell to pay."

"What was the last sighting of this beast, or were-cat, or whatever it is?"

"It wore up at Slawit Hall, last any of us heard. It killed the old man Bob Slawit and his grandson."

"It never killed Bob Slawit. That thing *is* Bob Slawit, he's the were-cat. I saw him change wi' me own eyes. One minute he was a man, just same as you and me, and t'next he'd changed into some'at 'orrible, from t'depths of hell. Covered in ginger fur he was, and big as a bull, and strong as an ox. He even had horns."

"Cats with 'orns? I always knew you were a daft bugger Charlie, but I never knew you were that bloody daft."

"Where else has this thing been seen, apart for Slawit Hall?"

"It wore in t'village here, rampaging through the high street where it killed five young men before it went up to Slawit Hall and killed Bob Slawit's grandson. Since then we haven't seen it, but there's some as say it killed some coppers before any of us ever saw it, and some as say they've heard it howling at night, and there's some as say they've seen it skulking up on Nobble Moor, looking for prey. My advice to you is to keep well away from it, whatever it is."

"Thank you for your advice gentlemen, you've been most helpful," said Banner, finishing his pint. "I think it's time I turned in. I've had a long day."

He stood up, picked up his two bags, and went up to his room.

"Who wore that clever bugger?" One of them asked after Banner had left.

"I don't know, but he's a southerner. Did you notice he never offered to buy a round? That's southerners for yer. I'll tell you some'at else, and all. I reckon he's come up here to interfere in some'at he knows nowt about."

"Well, if that is why he's here, he's in for a right bloody shock when that were-cat claps eyes on him. He won't know what's hit him if he gets in its way."

The three men nodded in agreement and picked up their pints of Nobblethwaite Best. Each of them took a very small sip of his drink, set his pint back on the table, and again nodded in unison with the others.

Early next morning, Banner hoisted himself from his bed, showered, dressed, and strapped on the shoulder hol-

ster for his Smith and Wesson model 29 classic Magnum
.44, along with the ankle holster for his Smith and Wesson .38 special, his backup sidearm. He checked the effect
in the mirror, and, satisfied that he wouldn't alarm the
locals by looking as if he was bearing firearms in public,
he went outside. It was a foggy morning, and the houses
further along the cobbled street were shrouded in mist,
giving them a ghostly quality.

Banner walked past them, leaving the small village behind, went up to the top of Nobble Hill, and saw Slawit
Hall for the first time.

It stood on its own in the mist, huge and menacing.
Behind it, he knew, hidden by the mist, was Nobble Moor,
a wilderness of rolling hills covered in grassy swamps and
patches of heather.

There was police tape around the doors of Slawit Hall,
but there were no police guarding the place. It seemed
they'd got whatever evidence they expected to find and
abandoned the crime scene. He ignored the tape, and,
pulling his Magnum .44 from its holster, he went inside.
He found himself in a classic entrance hall with panelled
walls and a grand staircase straight ahead. It was dilap-
idated and covered in cobwebs. Keeping his gun at the
ready, Banner advanced cautiously. Ahead of him on the
floor there was the chalk outline of a man, or at least of
part of a man. It looked as if he was missing his head, and
possibly an arm.

Banner inspected the entire house. There was no sign of
old man Slawit, or of the were-cat, or whatever it was that

had killed five young men in the village. Banner suspected it had been, if anything, a zomcat. He didn't know what zomcats might be able to do, but since this one had killed five young men, and possibly other victims, it had to be treated with the greatest respect.

He went back outside. The mist was rolling in from Nobble Moor and it was getting thicker. For Banner, this wasn't good news. It meant that if the zomcat put in an appearance, he wouldn't be able to see it until it was almost on him.

Keeping his gun at the ready, he made his way back along the drive to the cobbled street that led down the hill into Nobblethwaite. Before he got to the end of the drive, he saw an outline in the mist. He stopped and narrowed his eyes into slits.

It *was* a cat. A ginger cat.

He levelled his gun slowly, so as not to alert it to his presence, and took careful aim. It advanced towards him through the mist. He squeezed the trigger and blasted its head to Kingdom Come. The body of the cat remained on its feet for an instant without a head, then toppled sideways onto the drive.

Banner blew the smoke from the muzzle of his gun and slipped it into his holster. He walked up to the headless cat corpse and inspected it. He quickly realised that he hadn't destroyed a zomcat; he'd killed an ordinary ginger tom, somebody's beloved pet, no doubt. He shrugged and pulled his pistol out again, and cautiously made his way back to the village.

He called in at the village butcher's shop. Albert the butcher was proudly showing off his new mincing machine to one of the locals, by feeding a sheep's head into the hopper and watching as it emerged from a funnel as a pink mush with specks of white in it.

"Morning," said Banner.

Albert and the local both turned their heads and looked at him as if he was an alien, which, in a sense, he was.

"Can I help you?" Albert asked.

"Yes," said Banner. "I'd like five pints of cow blood and one of those joints you've got hanging up. I'd like to collect them at five o'clock today, please. But I'll pay you now."

Albert and the local man looked at each other before Albert tore himself away from his demonstration and opened his till.

"Twenty-five pounds please," he said.

"That's a bit steep isn't it?" Banner asked, as he handed over the cash.

"It's what you pay for quality products. We don't sell any of that supermarket rubbish around here."

"All right. See you at five o'clock."

Banner left.

"Bloody southerners," said Albert.

As dusk was falling, Banner pulled a chair over to the first-floor window of a bedroom in Slawit Hall, and sat in it. Through the window he had a good view of the edge of Nobble Moor. He'd sprinkled trails of cow blood across the moorland near to Slawit Hall. They led to the joint of meat he'd bought, which was positioned a good distance from the house, but still well within his line of sight.

He set his rifle on a tripod then trained it on the joint of meat.

Now, it was a question of remaining still and silent for hours on end, if necessary, while retaining his concentration.

Dusk turned to night. Banner could still see the joint of meat clearly because he was looking at it through a night-sight. He kept stock-still.

If the zomcat came sniffing around the meat, it would get its head blown off, just like the other unfortunate cat that had crossed Banner's path.

A shape disturbed the grass. It could have been a cat – or another small animal. Banner ignored it and kept his focus on the joint of meat. There was no point in alerting the zomcat by letting off a shot at something vague, which might not even be the zomcat. He wanted a clean shot at a quarry he could identify.

The only movement he made was that of his stomach and chest as he breathed, slowly and deeply, keeping his body in a state of relaxed readiness.

The sound of a cat's footstep is an almost legendary thing.

It's a by-word for the closest thing to silence that there can be.

Yet, so keen were Banner's ears, that he heard it.

An impossibly quiet, but distinct, pad, pad, pad, as a cat's feet stepped on the wooden floor behind him. He stood up quickly, picking up the rifle and spinning around with it in his hands, the tripod dangling from it. The cat leaped up at him and he pulled the trigger. The bullet took off a hind leg, and the cat landed on his chest, gripping his combat jacket with claws that could have been sharpened in hell. It lunged with open jaws for his face.

Banner dropped his rifle, got his hands around its neck, and squeezed for all he was worth. It did no good. The animal either didn't feel pain, or ignored it. He felt its remaining hind leg clawing at his belly, tearing strips from his jacket. For a small animal, it was possessed of an alarming strength. The thought crossed Banner's mind that he might not be able to keep it from biting his face for long. He kept hold of its neck with his left hand, while reaching inside his jacket with his right. As he did so, it wriggled almost free of his grip and lunged at him. He felt its teeth scrape against his chin and in the same instant he placed the muzzle of his Magnum .44 into its mouth and blew it away.

Some sort of vile fluid leaked from the headless body of the cat onto Banner's hands, just before it fell to the floor. He felt a burning sensation on his fingers. He rushed to the nearest bathroom and rinsed his hands under the tap. There was a mirror above the wash hand basin. Banner took a torch from his pocket and examined his face in the mirror. He had a tiny scar on his chin. What did that mean? Could he be infected with something?

He took his hunting knife from his belt and ruthlessly sliced off the flesh where he'd been scarred, hoping that he'd sliced it off in time to prevent any infection from spreading throughout his body. His blood flowed freely from the self-inflicted wound. He let it drop into the basin for a few minutes. Then, satisfied he'd done all he could to protect himself, he used his first-aid kit to dress the wound as best he could, and drove to the accident and casualty department of the Nab General Hospital.

After a wait of several hours he was finally seen by a doctor, who cleaned the wound with an antiseptic.

"I'm going to have to stitch this up," said the Doctor. "It'll be painful, unless I use a local anaesthetic."."

"Just get on with it. Don't bother with the anaesthetic, I'm in a hurry," said Banner.

"Are you sure?"

Banner nodded.

The Doctor widened his eyes and prepared his needle and thread. He carefully sewed up the wound, pulling the two sides of it together as best he could. Banner didn't flinch.

"Thanks," he said when the Doctor was done. "I'll be on my way now."

It was 10.00 a.m. by the time he got back to Nobblethwaite. He went to his room in the Ne'er Do Well and used his laptop to email a detailed report to his handler in MI5. When he'd done that, he packed his bags, put them in the back of his Land Rover, and began the long journey through miles of road works and cones back to London.

As he approached Leicester Forest East, Banner felt an odd sensation. It was a sensation that someone else might have missed, but Banner, being a trained man and an athlete, could discern immediately that all was not well. He decided he ought to take a break from driving, so he pulled off the motorway at the services and bought a black coffee from the Costa Coffee shop. He sat at a table by the window and began drinking his coffee. There was something wrong with it. It didn't quite taste the way it should.

Banner felt a tingling sensation to either side of his nose. He touched his hand to his cheek. There were what seemed to be several wires protruding from his skin. He quickly stood up and made his way to the toilets, noticing as he did that heads were turning on all the tables and looking at him as he moved amongst them to the toilet entrance. In fact, they were doing more than just looking at him; jaws were dropping in amazement, or something else – fear, perhaps.

Banner quickened his pace.

He got to the toilets and looked in the mirror. He'd grown a set of whiskers, like a cat, and in the time it'd taken him to get from his table to the toilet, he'd acquired a covering of short ginger fur all over his face.

The other men using the toilets were all looking at him, while trying to look as if they weren't looking at him. One of them managed to piss himself.

Banner found a vacant cubicle and locked himself in it. He pulled his mobile from his pocket and sent a text message:

My dearest Flagge, I have no choice. Please remember that, and please forgive me when news of what I've done reaches you. Above all, remember that I love you, now and forever, with all of my heart. All my love, Daddy xxx

He dropped the mobile which clattered on the tiles at his feet.

He took his Magnum .44 from its holster and stuck it in his mouth at an angle that would ensure that his brain would be thoroughly destroyed.

Then he did the right thing for Queen and country: he squeezed the trigger.

Chapter 6

The morning was cold and bright.

Iris Simpson boiled the kettle in the kitchen at the back of the small cottage she and her husband occupied near the top of South Stonker Lane, and made a flask of tea.

"Are you ready Brian?" She shouted.

"I am, luvie," he replied. "I've got me paper and I'm just getting me shoes and coat on."

Summer was turning to autumn, so they both made sure they were well-wrapped before venturing out and walking the short distance to the wooden bench down the road that overlooked the town of Huddersfield. The bench had a brass plaque on it which said: 'Queen's Jubilee Year 1977'.

They sat on the bench and Iris poured them both a cup of tea. The two pensioners liked to spend an hour sitting on this bench every day, weather permitting.

Brian unfolded the newspaper he'd been carrying and began reading it. It was the Huddersfield Examiner. The front page bore the headline: 'Zombie Festival Comes to Town'.

He read the story with a keen interest.

'Tarquin Camemblert, the prime Minister, let it be known today through official sources that there will be a series of festivals across the country in honour of the sacrifices made by the townspeople of Huddersfield, which enabled him to put paid to the plague of zombies which was on the verge of bringing the country to its knees. The theme of the festivals will be clog-dancing celebrity chef zombies. The main festival will be held in Huddersfield itself, in the town's famous St. George's Square, and will be attended by a number of visiting dignitaries including the Prime Minister and the President of the United States of America, Adolf Doughnut.

It is anticipated that the festival will bring much-needed funds into the town, that will help pay for the rebuilding of the town centre, which had to be bombed as part of the war effort against the zombies.'

Just as he got to the end of the paragraph, Brian felt a sharp object in his ribs. It was his wife's elbow. Then he heard her voice whispering in his ear.

"Brian, just look at that. There's some right funny looking people coming down our road."

Brian lowered his newspaper and peeped over the top of it.

"Don't make it so obvious, you bloody daft bugger," she said.

Somewhat confused, he raised the newspaper again, and peered around the side of it. He saw three people on the other side of the street. The first of them had a yellow skinned jaundiced look about him, and he had his black hair styled in a magnificent pompadour. The second would have been a strikingly attractive and exotic-looking woman with long jet-black hair, were it not for the fact that she, too, was yellow, which somehow gave the impression of decay; and the third was a burly type, with a bristling moustache, a similar yellow complexion, and the appearance of a bouncer at a cheap nightclub.

"They look like a right load of weirdos," said Iris. "I'll bet yer they're all immigrants, those three. Probably from somewhere in Eastern Europe."

The one with the pompadour turned his head, flashed a charming grin at the two pensioners, and waved at them, while directing his gaze into Brian's eyes, which were watching him at an odd angle necessitated by the newspaper he was holding.

"Nice day," he shouted, in a plummy accent. "I see you're both enjoying the sunshine."

Brian reddened. He thought he'd been very discrete. He waved back uncertainly, and watched the three-odd-looking people saunter further down the steep road.

"They didn't sound very foreign," said Brian.

"No, you're right. What the bloody hell was going on? Have you ever seen the like?"

"Wait a minute. I know exactly what it was. Look at this."

Brian held up the front page of his newspaper and pointed to the opening paragraph of the lead article.

"See that? They're having a festival in the town centre to raise money. They're getting folk dressed up as clog-dancing zombies to raise the money for us. I bet you those three are in fancy dress and they're on their way to a rehearsal for the festival."

"They weren't wearing clogs."

"Can you blame 'em? Clogs aren't right comfortable. They'll probably be putting their clogs on when they get to the rehearsal room."

"Aye, happen."

Iris poured another cup of tea and Brian got back to reading his newspaper. He felt another nudge in his ribs.

"Brian, we've got company," his wife said.

Brian looked up. The three odd-looking yellow people were standing in front of him and his wife.

The one with the flamboyant hairstyle spoke.

"Hello again," he said. "Please do excuse us for interrupting your time together. We couldn't help but notice the headline on your newspaper, and all three of us want to take a quick look at the front page, if you don't mind. Is that all right? We'll only be a minute."

Brian turned his head and looked at his wife for guidance as to whether he should mind or not. She shrugged, so he handed the newspaper over.

Floyd Rampant took it and stood reading it, with Fletcher and De Vine on either side of him, reading it at the same time as him.

When he finished, he removed the front page and returned the rest of the newspaper to Brian.

"I hope you don't mind if I keep this to study later, at my leisure," he said.

"Well, actually-"

"Don't say you won't let me take this one tiny little piece of your newspaper," Rampant said. "You'd hurt my feelings if you said that. And my friends don't like it when people hurt my feelings."

Fletcher and De Vine both glared at Brian.

"Well, when you put it that way, of course you can take it."

Iris opened her mouth to speak, but thought the better of it, and kept her feelings to herself.

"Thank you so much," Rampant said, pinching Brian's cheek. "You've been an absolute little gem. I'm ever so grateful. Toodle-oo."

He turned and led his two colleagues away.

Brian and Iris looked at each other and they both shrugged. Brian got back to his newspaper and iris poured them both another cup of tea.

"When are we going to get something to eat? I'm ravenous. Can't we go back and eat those two?" Fletcher asked.

"No, you silly-arse, we can't. If we eat someone in broad daylight, we'll be seen for sure, and before you know it, they'll be sending in the army to wipe us out again. We have to be more discreet than that," Rampant replied.

"What are we going to do then?"

"When we find somewhere suitable, we're going to collect some money for charity."

"What do you mean?"

"You'll see."

Chapter 7

Bob Trotter looked up from his desk, which was in front of a picture window. He lived in one of the few large houses that had been built near the top of South Stonker Lane to take advantage of the views it offered.

Through his window he could see most of Huddersfield sprawled out in the valley far below. It was a view that disturbed him these days, because it always reminded him that the centre of his beloved home town had been flattened by bombs during the military action that had wiped out the zombies.

He watched as people scurried amongst the rubble, operated diggers, and, in a few cases, erected scaffolding for the rebuild that would soon be taking place, money permitting.

He lowered his head and began writing again. Having retired the previous year, Bob had taken up writing as a hobby. He liked to write longhand then type it up later. Like every second person on the planet, he believed he had a novel in him, if only he could find it. So far it had proved elusive, but he persisted in looking for it. Having tried and failed to get anywhere with almost every conceivable genre, he'd decided on what was for him a radical approach: he was going to write about zombies.

He was halfway through a sentence on the first page when the doorbell rang. He stood up, left his study, walked through his small library, and then through the magnificent entrance hall to his front door. It was all kept immaculately clean due to the efforts of the cleaner he paid to do his cleaning every day of the week.

Trotter's front door had a decorative glazed panel set into it. The panel was translucent and it allowed him to see visitors, and allowed visitors to see him, but not very clearly. He peered through the glazed panel. He could tell that there were three people standing in the porch, but they were no more than shadowy figures, seen through a glass darkly. They were an odd colour, and he wasn't sure he liked the looks of them, insofar as he could see them at all. He was glad he had multiple locks and bolts on his front door.

"Who is it?" He asked.

A plummy voice answered:

"Charity clog-dancing celebrity chef zombies."

"Charity what?" Trotter asked.

"We're clog-dancing celebrity chef zombies. We're collecting money to help with the rebuilding of Huddersfield. We're part of the festival team."

Rampant pressed the front page of the Huddersfield Examiner against the glass panel on the front door, and Trotter looked closely at it. He read the headline and the first few paragraphs, and then he pressed his face against the panel so that he could get a better view of his visitors.

They looked like people dressed as zombies all right, and they were collecting for a cause close to his heart, the rebuilding of his home town.

Trotter undid the many bolts securing his front door, unlocked it, and pulled it open.

"You better come in," he said. "I'll see what I can give you."

His three visitors followed him in and Rampant shut the door behind them, and securing it with the bolts.

"No need for that," said Trotter. "You won't be staying long, after all."

"Oh, but we will," said Rampant. "This is our new home."

"What-what do you mean?"

"We were homeless until a few minutes ago. Now we've got a home. This is it. That's what I mean."

Trotter's jaw dropped.

"Perhaps you could take us on a guided tour and show us around our new home. We're very interested in everything about it, especially the kitchen."

Trotter felt his knees giving way. He forced himself to be brave.

I'll play along with them, he thought. Make them think I'm not going to take a step out of line. Then, as soon as they're off guard, I'll escape or call the police.

He led them up the generously proportioned staircase to the first floor of his house.

"This is the master bedroom," he said, opening a door.

"That'll be mine, then," said Rampant.

Trotter felt himself bridle. He made a sweeping gesture with his hand.

"These are the doors to the other bedrooms. All but one have en-suites, and there's a family bathroom for good measure. Let's go back downstairs now. This is the hall of course, library, my study where I do all my work, the lounge, drawing room, snug, kitchen, and utility room, and below this level there's a large basement and keeping room, and what was the coal cellar in days gone by. That's it."

"It's perfectly wonderful. My name's Floyd Rampant by the way, and these are my lovely associates, Kat De Vine and Gary Fletcher. Gary likes to be known as Gaz."

Rampant extended his hand.

"And you are?" He asked, with a smile on his face.

Against his better instincts, Trotter shook Rampant's hand, which he found to be rather cold.

"Bob Trotter. You can call me Bob."

"Splendid. Let's all be on first name terms. You can call be Floyd. Now then Bob, tell me a bit about yourself."

"Well, I'm retired," said Trotter. "And I live here alone."

He thought he might have made a mistake saying that, so he quickly added:

"I have a cleaner who comes every day, and my son often visits me, and my ex-wife sometimes drops in."

Rampant nodded while stroking his chin.

"A son, eh?" He said. "Perhaps you could show me a photograph of him."

Trotter's heart sank.

"I'm afraid I don't have any," he said.

"What? You don't have any photographs of your son? That's rather unusual isn't it, Bob? Most fathers would keep photographs of their sons close to hand, don't you think? I have a feeling you've been making things up, Bob. I'm right, aren't I?"

He gave Trotter a penetrating red-eyed stare.

Trotter gulped and nodded.

"There is no son, and no ex-wife either, is there Bob?"

"No. Sorry," said Trotter.

His mouth felt suddenly dry and he had trouble getting the words out.

Rampant grinned.

"Well, don't you worry," he said. "I'm going to be very understanding, as long as it doesn't happen again. Just behave yourself, and do as you're told from now on, and things will go well for you. But take one step out of line and you're going to end up in an awful big pickle. Or a stew."

De Vine and Fletcher both threw back their heads and laughed. Trotter had the feeling that a joke had been made at his expense, but he didn't quite get it.

"Yes," he said. "Of course, of course I'll behave myself and do as I'm told. You can count on me."

Rampant pinched Trotter's cheek.

"I always knew I could, Bob. Let's lay down a few ground rules, shall we? You're going to stay at home from now on, and act as if everything is normal. You're going to pretend you've decided to have three house guests. It's not really pretence, when you think about it, is it? The fact is that you *have* decided to take in three house guests, because the consequences of not doing so don't bear thinking about."

"No, I don't suppose they do."

"So that's your job. Our job is to make sure you do your job. It's as simple as that."

He thrust his face forward so that his nose was no more than an inch from Trotter's nose.

"Do you think you can handle the job I've just given you, Bob?"

Trotter nodded his head vigorously.

"Yes, yes, of course."

"That's perfectly splendid."

"I'm still ravenous. When are we going to eat?" Fletcher asked.

"This evening you two can go on a hunting expedition. I'll stay here and look after Bob."

"What will they be hunting?" Trotter asked.

"Fresh supplies of meat for our cooking pots."

"There's a halal butchers a quarter-mile down the road in Birkby, and you'll find a Tesco if you follow the road into town."

"We'll bear that in mind, but I think it's unlikely that either of them'll stock what we're after."

"The halal butcher is very good. He sometimes has mutton which is unusual for a butcher's shop in Huddersfield."

Rampant cocked his head to one side and grinned.

"We want the sort of meat that comes on two legs. He won't stock that."

"Two-legged meat? What do you mean?" Trotter asked.

Rampant grinned again and did a gesture with the index and middle finger of his right hand, making his hand look like a man taking a walk.

Trotter's jaw dropped.

"Get it now, do we Bob?"

Trotter felt faint. He turned and fled into his study. As he did so, he heard the peals of laughter of his three new guests ringing in his ears. He stared out of the window for a while, then sat down at his desk, and decided to submerge himself in his writing to take his mind off things. He picked up his pen and read the opening paragraphs of his new novel:

'Amos Crabtree cowered in his garage as his neighbour Terry Baldwick, whose funeral he had attended the previous Saturday, lumbered towards him with his arms outstretched, as if in expectation of an emotional reunion.

Amos had the disturbing feeling that his former neighbour was after more than a friendly hug, and looked around for a means of escape. Unfortunately, he was standing in the narrow corridor between the side of his car and the concrete wall of his garage, and he'd reversed his car close to the end wall of the garage, leaving no scope to run around the rear of it. There was no escape.

He put his hands on the roof of the car and scrabbled with his legs, trying to climb on top of it. He scratched the paintwork he'd been so proud of with his clumsy kicking, but accomplished little else.

Realising that he wasn't athletic enough to make it onto the roof of his car, Amos turned to face the apparition that was now only a couple of feet away.

His former neighbour was the last thing on earth he wanted to see, but nevertheless he blurted out:

"Terry, it's great to see you. How are you keeping?"

A second later, Baldwick's filth-encrusted arms embraced him. He smelled the rankness of Baldwick's undead body, and felt Baldwick's teeth sink into his cheek, tearing a strip of his face off. He tried to push his attacker away, but-'

Trotter ripped the page from his notebook, screwed it up, and threw it in the waste bin.

The three zombie chefs paced around Trotter's front room until night had fallen, then De Vine and Fletcher went out and walked down the hill into Birkby.

De vine, as usual, was very fetchingly dressed in a red boob-tube, a black leather mini-skirt, and black stockings. Her legs, which were long and shapely, looked longer and shapelier still due to the six-inch heels she was wearing. With each step she took, her hips swayed first one way, then the other.

Fletcher, by comparison, looked coarse and brutish, with his burly bouncer's physique, his squat frame, and his bristling black moustache.

Eventually they entered the outskirts of Birkby. The shops were all closed and few people were around. Fletcher hid in the shadows outside a shop on Grimscar Avenue, while De Vine stood at the edge of the pavement, and did her best to look interesting. It was something that required very little effort on her part; in fact, it came rather naturally to her.

Chapter 8

Quince Roper drove through the darkness towards the red-light district of Huddersfield with feelings of trepidation. He didn't usually feel this way. He'd always enjoyed his excursions to the area in the past. But recent events had brought about a change in the way he viewed it.

He'd picked up a 'whore' as he liked to call them, and gone back to her place on Canal Street. He'd agreed on the service she'd provide, then he'd slapped her around a bit to make things more interesting, as he liked to think of it. Usually when he did this, he'd be able to offer his victim more money to shut her up, but the last time, he hadn't been so lucky. She'd started mouthing off and threatening to go to the police. There'd been a scene, and she'd ended up dead.

That was six months ago. Somehow, he'd managed to avoid being caught, or even questioned by the police. As a family man with an impeccable middle-class pedigree, he wasn't an obvious suspect.

For six months he'd stayed away from the area. He'd gone to other towns to satisfy his needs. But that involved a drive, and he hadn't got time tonight for a long drive. He needed dick action, and he needed it quick.

As Roper approached the viaduct near Garrard's Timber Yard where he knew some of the girls would be plying their trade, he wondered if he should be doing this. He'd abused quite a few of them. What if one of them recognised him, remembered what he'd done to her, and tipped off the police? What if she were to take a photo of him with her mobile and show it to the police?

That was the trouble with modern technology. There was always the possibility of a photograph being taken of you, or – heaven forbid – a video, when you least wanted it.

These concerns began preying on his mind and at the last minute he turned down a side-street, took a couple more turns, and headed away from the viaduct. He couldn't risk it. But he was horny as hell. What could he do? He considered stopping his car in a quiet lay-by and tossing himself off, but that was a last-resort in Roper's view, and wouldn't, in any case, satisfy his cravings for violence with his sex. There was always his wife, but she'd threatened to go to the police when he'd tried his tricks on her a couple of decades ago.

Whichever way he looked at it, he had no alternative but to go out of town. But he couldn't do that, not tonight. The pressure inside him was building up. It needed relieving quickly.

He drove in no particular direction, hoping he might see someone, anyone, who he could coax into his car, and cart off somewhere quiet. It didn't have to be a whore, in fact it might be better if she wasn't; more satisfying, somehow. Funny how he'd never thought of that before.

He drove up Halifax Old Road, cursing at the speed bumps, took a left turn, and found himself driving along

Grimscar Avenue. The place seemed deserted. He slowed down, hoping there might be a woman going somewhere on her own.

That was when he saw her.

A startling vision of beauty.

She had black hair, cut-glass cheekbones, and a face that was somehow haughty. She was tall, at least six foot, and the way she was dressed left little to the imagination. Even so, his imagination began working overtime. She saw him driving towards her and smiled at him. Roper couldn't believe his luck.

That's a come-on if ever there was one, he thought.

He imagined what he would do to her, and how he would do it. Images of the woman's haughty face pleading for mercy flashed through his mind.

He pulled up next to her, wound down the side window of his car, and leaned towards her.

"Are you looking for business, love?" He asked.

"Yes," she purred. "What would you like?"

He looked her up and down.

"Everything you do," he said. "What would you charge?"

They negotiated and struck up a deal for De Vine's services. She opened the passenger door and climbed in. The driver put his hand on the handbrake to release it. She covered his hand with hers and stopped him from doing so.

"Not so fast, Mister," she said.

His eyes widened. He was shocked at how strong she was. He heard the rear door of his car open and turned his head to see Fletcher getting into the back of his car.

"Now just hang on a -" he said.

Fletcher got hold of the man's neck and squeezed it between his finger and thumb.

"You hang on," he said. "You're going to do exactly as we say, or your head is going to look very silly, because it's going to be flopping around at the end of a broken neck. Turn your car around and drive back the way you've come."

Roper did as he was told.

De Vine put her hand on his thigh.

"There's a good boy," she breathed. "You and I are going to have a good time tonight, if you just do as you're told."

Roper felt himself getting aroused and scared at the same time. He was pretty sure that De Vine's idea of a good time wasn't quite the same as his idea of a god time.

My steering lock's in the foot well, he said to himself. I'll grab it first chance I get and whack them both with it. Then I'll show the bitch what's what. I'll show her who orders who around.

The thought comforted him.

"Turn left here," said Fletcher, when they reached the T-junction at Halifax Old Road. "Then take the first right turn you come to."

The right turn was South Stonker Lane. When they were about half-way up it, Fletcher said:

"Stop here and leave the engine running."

Roper obediently pulled up and De Vine got out of the car.

"Get out," said Fletcher.

Roper knew it was now or never. He reached into the foot well, grabbed his steering lock, and leapt out of the car taking the two zombies by surprise.

"Come on," he said, whirling around and swinging the steering lock as if it was a medieval weapon, "I'll fucking take both of ya on."

Fletcher opened the back door of the car and climbed out, quite unhurriedly. Roper took up a guard position with the steering lock raised above his head, ready to meet Fletcher's attack. But Fletcher didn't attack him. Instead, he got casually into the front of the car and wound down the window.

"See you later, Kat," he said, and drove off.

Roper was left holding his makeshift club over his head, and wondering how he could get his car back. Kat smiled at him.

"You seem jumpy," she said. "Whatever is the matter?"

"You know damned well what the matter is. Your friend has just stolen my car and I fucking well want it back."

"He's only borrowed it. He'll bring it back, and in the meantime you and I could get to know each other. How about it, big boy?"

Roper slowly lowered the steering lock.

The woman was a funny sort of colour – he could see that now, even in the darkness - but at the end of the day, she was only a woman, so he surely had nothing to fear from her. He could play along, wait till they were safely off the street, overpower her in private and have a little fun at her expense. Fun of the sort she wouldn't expect or appreciate. Then, when her friend showed up with the car, he'd get what was coming to him, which was at the very least concussion, courtesy of the steering lock.

"That's better," said Kat, when she saw him relax.

She sauntered over to him and linked his arm.

"You're coming with me," she said, and Roper felt himself getting excited about what was to come.

She led him through an impressive gateway, down a path to a magnificent house, and put her mouth close to the side of his head.

"This is where I live," she said, and she stuck her tongue briefly in his ear.

Trotter found her presence intoxicating, and the thought of what they might do, and what he might do to her, even more intoxicating.

"Does your friend live here with you?" Roper asked.

"No," said Kat. "He lives down the road."

She opened the door and gently pulled Roper in. He didn't quite trust her, so he clutched the steering lock in his free hand in case he needed a weapon.

They went inside. The place was quiet.

"No point in putting off the inevitable," said Kat, unlinking Roper's arm and taking hold of his hand, "Come with me to my bedroom. We'll get refreshments later."

She pulled him upstairs, but, to be fair, he didn't need much pulling. He bounded up the steps behind her. They entered the bedroom and Roper threw off his clothes. Kat took off her boob tube and skirt. She was wearing only her heels and scanty knickers.

"I like to be on top," she said.

Roper grabbed hold of her hair.

"If anyone's going to be on top, it's me," he said.

But he was wrong.

In an instant he found himself on his back, on the bed, with Kat on top of him. She somehow wriggled out of her panties and then came his worst nightmare.

At least, he thought it was his worst nightmare until Fletcher entered the room.

"I don't normally do this sort of thing, you know," said Fletcher, "but any port in a storm and all that."

Again, he thought *this* was his worst nightmare until Rampant entered the room.

After that, Kat looked at his groin and licked her lips.

And somehow he knew that she wasn't thinking about pleasuring him.

Chapter 9

Roper had looked after himself. He was lean and muscular – and far too big to fit in a single stew-pot. Rampant made several other dishes from him in addition to the stew, some of which were cooked in the oven and some of which were done in a frying pan. When he finished each dish, he carefully dolled it out, ensuring that he and his two companions all got the same amount.

By the time they'd finished eating Roper, they'd each had a substantial meal, but they were still hungry.

"What now?" Fletcher asked, tilting back his head while sucking the marrow from a thigh-bone.

"We lie low," said Rampant, "we regroup, and we plan. And sooner or later, we claim the world for our own."

Fletcher belched loudly.

"I meant, what are we eating next?"

"Oh, I see. You and Kat can go out hunting again. See if you can bag a couple, next time. I'll get Bob to do the washing up."

Chapter 10

It was late evening and Henderson was prowling around the houses on South Stonker Lane. His instincts, or possibly his amazing sense of smell, propelled him in the direction of one house in particular.

Chapter 11

There was a meowing at the door. Rampant got up and opened it.

"Oh my goodness, it's so good to see you again," he said.

Floyd Rampant stood back and allowed Henderson to enter, then he closed the door. Henderson rubbed himself around Floyd's legs.

"You remember me, don't you, boy? Where have you been, you naughty thing? Do you know, I haven't said anything to my friends, but I've been worried sick about you. Anyway, it's your lucky day, follow me."

Rampant walked down the corridor into the kitchen and Henderson followed, meowing loudly.

Fletcher and De Vine were sitting at the dining table eating, while Bob Trotter was mopping the floor clean of blood with a glum expression on his face.

"Is there any of that stew left? The whatsit stew?" Rampant asked.

"Do you mean the Ainsley-Dyson stew? There's stacks. They were both big blokes," said Fletcher.

Rampant glanced at the hob. There was a huge cooking pot on it with a thick liquid simmering in it and appetising bones sticking up out of it. Several more cooking pots were lined up along the worktop, all of them brim-full.

"Good," he said. "I'm going to give some to my little friend here."

"Where did he come from?"

"I don't know. I suppose he ran off when they bombed St George's Square, but you know what cats are like. They get wanderlust. They can go missing for weeks and even months and then turn up out of the blue."

He looked fondly at Henderson.

"That's right, isn't it? You chaps are very naughty sometimes, aren't you?"

He took a small bowl from a kitchen cupboard then put it back and took out a large pasta bowl instead and used a ladle to fill it with Ainsley-Dyson stew, making sure that he scooped up a good few lumps of meat into it. While Rampant was preparing the bowl of stew, Henderson reached up with his forelegs so that his front paws were on Rampant's right hip, his claws digging into the fabric of Rampant's cream linen suit, while his hind paws remained in contact with the floor.

"Meow meow meow."

"For goodness sake, be patient you little devil. You really have very little in the way of manners. Do you know that?"

Rampant set down the pasta bowl and Henderson stuck his head in it, quickly lapping up the delicious juices and taking the lumps of meat in his mouth one by one, and chewing them with his head held sideways as he did so. He made little growling noises of pleasure while he ate.

"Do you know, boy, you sound just like my friend Gaz does, when he's eating. He doesn't have any manners either," said Rampant.

Kat laughed loudly and Fletcher rolled his eyes.

When Henderson had finished eating, Rampant picked him up and carried him into the front room. He settled down with Henderson on his lap and used the remote to switch on the television. After a while, Kat and Fletcher joined him, leaving Trotter to clear away their dirty plates and do the washing up. Henderson purred loudly and nodded off. After a while he woke up and jumped off Rampant's lap. The lounge door was slightly ajar. Henderson pushed it open with his nose then squeezed through into the hall and stood by the front door, meowing loudly.

"What does he want this time?" Kat asked.

"He wants to go out," Rampant replied.

He went to the door and opened it, and Henderson left to resume his adventures.

Chapter 12

Prime Minister Camemblert looked up and frowned. The Times crossword was, as usual, proving too difficult for him. He threw the Times into the bin and opened the Sun, a down market tabloid with a considerably easier crossword to solve. He soon fathomed the clue for one across.

"That's better," he said to himself, as he pencilled in the answer.

He was busy mulling over the next clue when the door to his office burst open and his aide Johnson came in.

"Can't you bloody well knock, Johnson?" He demanded, hiding his newspaper behind a pile of official documents. "I was in the middle of something important."

"Sorry Prime Minister, but I've got urgent news for you."

The PM sighed.

"As if I don't have enough on my plate already, without having urgent news to contend with. All right, what is it, Johnson?"

Johnson's face looked unsure of what expression it should adopt.

"Good news and bad news, Prime Minister," he said.

Camemblert frowned.

"I always hate it when people say that. The bad news is always bloody awful, and the good news is slightly less bloody awful. I suppose it's traditional to ask for the

217

bad news first. I'm sitting down. You might as well tell me what's gone on. What is it? Another opinion pollster claiming that the opposition is trouncing us again?"

"No, something worse than that Prime Minister."

"A backbench revolt?"

"Worse even than that."

"A leadership bid by one of my rivals?"

Johnson shook his head.

"Well, that's reassuring," said the PM. "The one thing I wouldn't be able to stand is one of my colleagues ousting me from power and crowing that he'd got one over on me. I can take anything but that. Well, anything but that and physical pain. What's happened, exactly?"

Johnson tightened his upper-lip, British public school-style.

"It's Banner, Prime Minister. Flagg Banner. He's dead."

"What?" asked the PM. "Banner dead? Why didn't any-body tell me about this before?"

"We've only just found out."

"Fuck me pink. What about the bloody zomcat?"

"That's the good news, Prime Minister. Banner de-stroyed the zomcat before he killed himself."

"Killed himself? You mean he committed suicide?"

"Yes, it's tragic really. He blew out his brains in a toilet cubicle in the Leicester Forrest services just off the M1. As far as we can see, he'd been drinking a black coffee then he just went and blew his own head off. There's a theory that the cat bit him and infected him with the zombie virus, and that's why he took his own life. He was a brave man. He did the right thing."

"He did. And we're going to do the right thing."

"What do you mean, Prime Minister?"

"We're going to give him a bloody good send off and make sure that everyone has a bloody good knees-up. You know the sort of thing I mean. Get one of the civil servants to organise it."

"Very good Prime Minister."

"You know, I'm quite relieved Johnson. For a minute, there I thought you were going to tell me that the zomcat was still on the loose and that I'd have to re-think the President's visit. But now I know it's been destroyed, the presidential visit can go ahead just as planned. Happy days."

Johnson turned to leave.

"Wait a minute, I've just had a thought."

Johnson paused.

"In order to make absolutely sure that nothing goes wrong, let's get the wonks on it. Bring them in here right away, will you? I want a word with them."

"Very good, Prime Minister."

"Hang on, there's something else!"

Johnson raised his eyebrows surreptitiously and turned to face the P.M.

"On second thoughts, don't get them all in here; just get the ones who I'll be able to talk to without needing an interpreter to explain what they say."

The wonks were the super-intelligent people who'd all got first-class honours degrees from Oxford and Cambridge, and gone straight into politics without first experiencing anything remotely resembling real life. They were at the forefront of originating and implementing government policy.

"Very good, Prime Minister."

Johnson rounded up the dozen or so wonks from Whitehall who, unlike their colleagues, could speak in something that resembled the English language and herded them into the PM's office. The PM had never seen a wonk before, and he was startled by their alien appearance. They were, to a man (and woman), thin and spotty, with thick spectacles and ridiculously high foreheads. Amongst their number there was one of black descent and one of Asian descent. Both of them conformed to the wonk stereotype.

The PM stood up and adjusted his tie. Then he jutted out his jaw, as he thought it gave him gravitas and authority, and began to speak.

"Right then," he said. "You lot probably know that the American President is paying our country a visit in a few days' time. We're going to have a fantastic shindig for him here at Westminster then we're going to take him up to Huddersfield for the centrepiece of his visit: a northern zombie clog-dancing festival. Nothing can be allowed to go wrong, or we'll all have egg on our faces, and there's nothing worse than getting egg on your face, unless it's getting it on your best shirt and your wife finds out. Right Johnson?"

"Right, Prime Minister."

"So I want you lot all to leave your normal duties for the time being, and concentrate on the Presidential visit. What I want you to do is to make sure that there is no scope whatsoever for anything to go wrong with the President's visit. If anything did go wrong, heaven forbid, he'd be gloating about it at my expense, and I want to be the one who's gloating at *his* expense. Is that clear?"

One of the wonks picked his nose. Another squeezed one of his many zits. The rest of them seemed to be looking at the ceiling or the floor.

The PM raised his voice.

"Have any of you listenEd to a damned word I've been saying?"

The wonks looked at him as if they'd noticed him for the first time, and nodded in unison.

"All right, clever dicks. What did I just say?"

They put up their hands.

"Right," said the PM, looking at each one in turn.

"You, you boy," he said. "The spotty one in the front row with the spectacles."

All the wonks in the front row immediately stuck their hands up.

"Bloody hell, this is no good, no good at all. Let's try again. Er, the spotty one with the spectacles who picked his nose."

All the airborne hands except one were lowered.

"Please sir," said the wonk who'd picked his nose. "You said you want us to leave our normal duties for the time being and concentrate on the Presidential visit. You want us to make sure that there is no scope whatsoever for anything to go wrong with his visit. If it did, heaven forbid, he'd be gloating about it at your expense, and you want to be the one who's gloating at *his* expense."

"Very good," said the Prime Minister. "Now I want you all to go back to your office in Whitehall and get to work."

The wonks filed out.

"That went rather well Johnson," said the PM after they'd left. "In fact, I feel as if I'm on a roll. I've wiped out the zombies, I've got rid of that pesky zomcat, and now I can enjoy being Prime Minister and lording it over my rivals. Best of all, I can be condescending to the American President while he's over here. Life doesn't get better than that."

Chapter 13

The wonks were a hard-working lot. They got busy drawing up policy proposals, guidelines, regulations, and directives, which they compiled into fifty spiral-bound A4 sized folders, each of them several hundred pages in length. These were boxed up and despatched to Huddersfield to provide guidance to Kirklees Council to make sure that nothing could go wrong during the presidential visit.

The wonks had thought of anything and everything, up to and including interference from zomcats, and had put in place measures to ensure that nothing, not even a plague of zomcats, could possibly derail the President's sojourn.

Chapter 14

Snark Hunter went home just as dawn was breaking. It was six o'clock in the morning and he'd been up all night beast-hunting, but he didn't go to bed. He went straight to his PC.

Hunter was a fifty-year-old loner who'd spent the last two decades of his life in pursuit of the Beast of Bodmin Moor, the legendary animal that is said to live on remote moorland in Cornwall, England.

Some said that the Beast was like a large cat, while others compared it to a panther. Only one thing was certain: that apart from the odd paw-print and grainy photograph, no-one had produced any concrete evidence that the Beast existed.

Hunter had made it his life's mission to get hold of hard evidence of the Beast's existence and proudly show it off to the world.

As soon as he was in front of his PC he made a series of internet searches for reported sightings of the Beast. He did this often, as he believed that any mention of it could prove to be a valuable lead which would enable him to achieve his life's ambition.

For once, he struck gold. There had been sightings of an animal in a village called Nobblethwaite which was up in Yorkshire. The animal had been variously described as a 'big cat', a 'puma', a 'were-cat', and – most tellingly of all – 'the Beast of Nobble Moor'. More recently, there had been a series of unexplained deaths in Nobblethwaite, and subsequently in the northern town of Huddersfield.

Hunter immediately realised that the sightings and the deaths were probably related, and suspected that that there was a Beast – perhaps the Beast of Bodmin Moor it-self – that had wreaked havoc in Nobblethwaite, and was now doing the same thing in Huddersfield.

He looked closely at Google Maps of the area and pinpointed the locations of the unexplained deaths in Huddersfield. He saw that they had all taken place near Stonker edge. The Edge was cheek-by-jowl with Stonker Moor, beyond which lay Nobble Moor and the village of Nobblethwaite.

The geography convinced Hunter that the Beast had made its lair somewhere near Stonker Edge and must be venturing into the town at night to wreak havoc.

Exhausted from lack of sleep, but fired up with excite-ment at the thought he might at last come face-to-face with the Beast, Hunter packed some food, clothing, and equipment in an old camper van he had on his drive be-fore setting off towards the north.

His camper van could do no more than fifty miles per hour, but since that was the fastest speed anyone could travel on the M5 and the M6 due to the many roadworks, that wasn't a problem.

It took him until 2.00 a.m. to reach Huddersfield, by which time he felt too tired to go any further. He pulled into a lay-by, climbed into the small bed he had in the back of his camper van, and slept.

At 9.00 a.m. he somehow managed to rouse himself and eat some breakfast, and he set off again. Soon he was driving up South Stonker Lane, the road leading up to Stonker Edge. It was so steep that he had to use the first gear of his ageing van all the way up it. Travelling at a speed which was not a great improvement on walking pace, he passed two pensioners sitting on a bench. One of them peered up from behind a newspaper to watch him driving by.

When Hunter reached the top of the hill he headed in the direction of Stonker Edge Farm, keeping his eyes peeled for likely-looking hideouts for a beast. He noticed that the fields around the farm were overgrown with wild grasses and weeds, and there was neither cattle nor crop to be seen anywhere on any of them.

Hunter had grown up on a farm and he knew what a well-kept farm should look like. It was obvious to him that something was wrong. The farm was either derelict, or – he hardly dared think it – the farmer had been killed by the Beast, and he had stumbled upon its lair.

He found a muddy track leading to the farmhouse. It was gated and guarded by an intimidating sign with skull and crossbones on it. The sign bore the words: 'Private. Keep Out. Trespassers will be prosecuted – if they survive being shot.'

Hunter left his camper van, opened the gate, and drove through. At the end of the track he came to a cobbled farmyard on which he parked his van. On one side of the yard stood the farmhouse. Opposite that, there was a barn and between them there were a few outbuildings and a tractor.

He climbed from his van and peered through the windows of the farmhouse. It looked spotlessly clean inside, and yet the farm itself had been allowed to go to rack and ruin. It was as if the farmer had gone on a long holiday. But that wasn't possible; farmers didn't take holidays.

He stepped away from the window and looked around.

Was it possible that the owner had died, and the place had been put up for sale by a relative who wasn't interested in farming? Hunter couldn't see any sale signs anywhere. Nevertheless, he made a quick online check using his mobile phone and quickly eliminated the possibility the farm was up for sale.

He concluded that it was highly likely that the farmer had become a victim of the Beast.

It occurred to him that he might become the next victim if he wasn't careful, so he took his illegally-owned shotgun from his camper van, loaded it, and began to explore.

He headed in the direction of the outbuildings. As he approached them, he noticed stains on the side of the tractor. They were faint, having been weathered somewhat, but he was still able to recognise them as bloodstains. He searched the area around the tractor methodically and found pieces of tattered clothing and chips of white matter which he assumed must be bone.

His heart began to beat faster.

He opened the doors of each of the outhouses in turn and looked inside. They were all empty.

Finally, he headed for the barn. He had good feelings about the barn. His instincts told him that if he was going to find the Beast anywhere, it would be there.

The barn had two enormous wooden doors set in an arch. There was a smaller, normal-sized door set into one of the big doors, which was open.

Hunter stood in front of the opening and peered inside. It was too dark to see anything.

He detected a movement in the darkness and levelled his shotgun. Then he felt something he hadn't expected to feel: fear. He forced himself to breathe deeply in order to settle his nerves and stepped back, so that whatever was lurking in the barn wouldn't be able to take him by surprise.

He saw it again, a subtle movement in the darkness.

Then the thing in the barn came so close that he was able to see it.

It was a cute little tabby cat.

Hunter relaxed and laughed out loud.

All that panic over a cat, he thought. I nearly blew its head off. How stupid of me to imagine that the beast was in there.

Moments later, more cats emerged from the barn. Three of them caught his eye: a huge black one, a ginger one almost as big, with a midsection that was flat and serrated at the edge; and a grey one which had carbon-fibre blades where it should have had hind legs.

The truth dawned on Hunter: he had found the Beast.

But there wasn't just one Beast; there was a horde of them, and they were taking an unhealthy interest in him.

He raised his weapon, chuckling despite his fear at the discovery that the Beast was very different from what he'd expected it to be.

"Right, you little basta-"

That was when Henderson landed on his head and Goliath took him by the legs. He fell off balance while pulling the trigger of his shotgun, discharging it harmlessly into the air. Then he fell to the ground where he became nothing more than a plate of high-quality cat-food, as fresh, appetizing, and irresistible as a field full of catnip.

The undead felines swarmed over him, biting lumps from his limbs, head and torso. Their attack was so ferocious that he was unable to put up any meaningful resistance. As his life ebbed away, Snark Hunter somehow found the strength to mumble a few mysterious and haunting last words:

"In the midst of the word he was trying to say,
In the midst of his laughter and glee,
He had softly and suddenly vanished away –
For the Snark was a Boojum you see."

Mercifully, he didn't survive the attack for long.

Chapter 15

Owen Blackhead was puzzled. He had two cats, neither of which had left the house for several days, which was most unlike them. Their names were Muthah and Fuckah. These were Owen's names for them; his wife and children called the cats Belle and Marmalade.

Muthah and Fuckah were lazy little sods at the best of times, but they were normally up to making the modest effort required to go outside once in a while. Or they had been until recently. What had changed? Perhaps they just needed a little encouragement.

Owen scooped up Muthah and carried her downstairs. He took her to the door leading from the basement kitchen to the back garden and opened it.

Immediately he'd done so, the cat began to struggle as if possessed. Despite his best efforts, he couldn't put her down where he wanted. She squirmed, wriggled, scratched, and bit, all the while meowling, until he was forced to let go of her. The animal fled upstairs quicker than he'd ever seen her move before.

He repeated the manoeuvre with Fuckah, with the same result.

It seemed obvious to Owen there must be something outside that the cats were afraid of, but what? He went into the back garden and looked around. There was nothing he could see that was out of the ordinary. Then he walked around the edge of the garden, carefully inspecting the fence and the privet hedge.

That was when he saw it.

Lying under the privet was the skeleton of a small animal. He guessed it was a cat. Something had eaten it, probably an urban fox, Owen reckoned. It had consumed most of the bones as well as the meat, skin and fur. It must have been a very hungry fox.

Owen got his garden spade and buried the remains in the hope that this might improve matters, but it didn't. The cats still wouldn't venture outdoors.

Too bad, he thought. Anyway, the fox won't be here forever. Sooner or later it'll go, and when it does, the cats will start going outdoors again.

Then he thought again about the remains he'd seen.

No, it couldn't have been a fox that did that, he decided. The bones were picked too clean for it to have been a fox. And the cats wouldn't be scared of a fox; we've had foxes before and they didn't give a monkey's about them. What could it really be that's scaring the cats?

He cast his eyes towards Stonker Edge, the grassy and near vertical slope which reared up on the other side of the valley, overlooking his house. It was one of the most commanding heights of Huddersfield. Then he remembered the were-cat he'd seen in Nobblethwaite, the village which lay on the other side of the moors beyond Stonker Edge, and shuddered. For some reason, it occurred to him to wonder whether the were-cat had anything to do with the skeletal remains he'd just buried. He quickly dismissed the idea.

Bob Slawit, the Beast of Nobble Moor, or were-cat, or whatever he was, couldn't be responsible for the dead cat. Still, Owen felt troubled by the thought.

He returned indoors wondering whether the fear that had infected his cats could be contagious, and whether he might have caught it.

When he got back upstairs he found the Huddersfield Examiner waiting for him on his doormat. He picked it up and went to his lounge, while reading the headline on the front page: "More Men Missing - FEARED Dead." It screeched.

Sensationalist horseshit, thought Owen. Nevertheless, he read the story.

"Quince Roper was the first to disappear.

Next, Bert Fossett was killed by an unknown assailant in his own back garden in Birkby. It seems his attacker could have been an animal. Some are suggesting he was killed by the Beast of Nobble Moor. A spokeswoman for the West Yorkshire Constabulary says the police regard this theory as highly unlikely but they are keeping an open mind about it. In the meantime, anyone with any information should call the number at the end of this article immediately to discuss the matter.

Shortly after Fossett's disappearance, Barbados Jones went missing. A neighbour reported seeing a dried bloodstain on the pavement near Jones's house, lending weight to the theory that the Beast of Nobble Moor may have claimed a second victim. Unfortunately, by the time the police forensic team arrived on the scene, there had been heavy rainfall, and the municipal road cleaner had been at work in the area, with the result that the forensic team could find nothing to assist the police investigation. Jones's sudden disappearance remains, for now, an unexplained mystery.

Equally puzzling are the disappearances of John Ainsley and Andrew Dyson.

But perhaps the most puzzling and disturbing of all these events is the fate of two men, Adrian Broadbent and Paul Formby, both whom worked for Acme TV repairs and Rentals Ltd. Their bodies have never been found, but in a shock development echoing the circumstances of Barbados Jones's possible demise, bloodstains were discovered in a shed at the Cemetery Road allotment in Birkby. Police analysis has established that the bloodstains were made by the blood of the two missing men, but their bodies have not been found.

Intriguingly, it seems the shed was used for the breeding of rats, and traces of organic rat and cat matter have been found in the shed, leading to speculation that the men may have been devoured by rats, or by cats, or even – however unlikely it may seem – the Beast of Nobble Moor."

Despite his doubts, Owen began to wonder if it was indeed possible that Blind Bob Slawit, whom he knew beyond shadow of a doubt to be the Beast of Nobble Moor, could have trekked across the moor and begum wreaking his terrible brand of havoc on the citizens of Huddersfield. Perhaps he could.

If that was the case, then perhaps Owen could get a video of Slawit turning into the Beast, or at least attacking someone while he was the Beast, and this would silence the many doubters who were making life unbearable for Owen, by posting mocking comments on his blog.

He looked out of his window at the sinister slope of Stonker Edge rearing up into the sky.

It must be him, he thought. An urban fox might have been capable of killing that cat in my back garden, but it couldn't have done for Fossett and Jones, and Broadbent and Formby and the others. And if the police knew what I knew, they'd be taking the Beast of Nobble Moor theory a lot more seriously than they are doing. I know Bob Slawit is a were-cat, and he's behind the disappearances. What's more, I'm going to prove it. I've got time on my hands. I'm in-between jobs right now. This is the perfect opportunity to show the world that I'm not a lunatic.

He put on his walking jacket and was about to go out when his wife Kylie saw him.

"Where are you going?" She asked.

"I'm just popping out for a walk," he replied.

"Where are you really going?"

"What do you mean?"

"Come on, Owen, I can always tell when you're not telling me the truth. What are you up to?"

"All right, you know that thing I told you about - Bob Slawit in the village of Nobblethwaite – the old bloke who became a shape-shifting were-cat? I think he's crossed over the moors. I think he's lurking somewhere up on top of Stonker Edge, and he's coming down at night and attacking people around here. It makes perfect sense."

"Owen, I'm beginning to worry about you. You've become obsessed with Slawit and were-cats. I want you to drop the subject before you go too far, and – and -"

"And, what?"

"I didn't want to say this, but now I'm going to have to: get yourself sectioned, that's what. Honestly, Owen, you should hear yourself speak. I could just about put up with it before, when you were going on about the Beast of Nobble Moor killing folk far away in Nobblethwaite somewhere, but now that you've started imagining it's here in Birkby, well, all I can say is: please don't tell our friends, and definitely don't post about it in your blog. Do you remember what happened last time you did that?"

"Of course I remember," he said. "And no, I'm not going to tell our friends or post about this. But I think I ought to be able to at least expect my own wife to back me, even if nobody else does. I'm going. Goodbye."

Owen left, slamming the door shut behind him. Kylie sighed. She hoped to God her man was going to be all right, and that he wasn't coming down with anything. Incipient madness, for instance.

Owen tramped crossly up the garden path, turned left along Poshton Avenue, and headed down the hill into the middle of Birkby. The leafy and genteel area he lived in with large detached and semi-detached houses soon gave way to streets of small terraced houses packed together, and the occasional cobbled street.

He walked amongst them until he came to Bert Fosset's house, a small terraced property with an unusually large back garden. He didn't know what he expected to find there, but he saw little more than a ring of police crime-scene tape cordoning it off from the other properties. He trekked the streets some more and found the area of paving outside 51, Bleardale Avenue that was said to have been smeared with the blood of Barbados Jones. He saw no trace of it.

Finally, he walked to the allotment on Cemetery Road where Adrian Broadbent and his young apprentice Paul Formby had met their terrible end. He soon identified Broadbent's shed, which was bigger and better than the ramshackle constructions built by the other allotment-owners, and was surrounded by yellow and black police tape.

He ventured as close as he could to the shed and peered at it. He wondered if he might find cat footprints in the soft earth nearby. Then he thought: even if I do, what will that prove? Only that a cat has been prowling around the place. I won't know if it was a were-cat.

He turned to leave, and found himself face to face with a grey-haired middle-aged man who was wearing, somewhat inappropriately given the autumnal sky, a white cheesecloth shirt and cream linen pants. He had a brown leather satchel slung over one shoulder and a notebook in his hands. He was making copious notes in the notebook. He looked up from his work.

"Good day to you, sir," he said, with a distinctly French accent. "Jaques Lay-zyoom at your service."

"Oh, hello," Owen replied, unsure of what to make of the fact that he'd just bumped into a note-taking Frenchman in the middle of an allotment in Birkby, Huddersfield.

"I'm Owen Blackhead. I'm very pleased to meet you."

He hesitated for a moment, and then extended his hand, as he thought it was the polite thing to do.

"I cannot shake hands monsieur," said the Frenchman. "I am busy taking notes, as you can zee."

"Oh, yes, of course. What are your notes about?"

"Zee murders of course. I am a detective, and I am here to solve these terrible crimes."

"You've come all the way from France to do that?"

"That I have sir, and with God's help, and with the science of logic, solve them I will."

"Amazing. How did you get to hear about the goings-on in Huddersfield when you live in France? Are you related to one of the victims?"

"I am a detective and I have my ways, sir."

"Which murders are you investigating exactly? I assume its Broadbent and Formby you're interested in."

"Not just those. There are Fossett and Jones as well, and others, are there not?"

"How do you know they were murdered? The victims might have just, I don't know, had a series of accidents."

"As I said, I am a detective and I have my ways, sir."

"I hope you don't mind me asking you something. I'm curious about what's been going on myself. There are suggestions that some kind of animal killed them all. Do you think that's possible?"

"Anything is possible, Monsieur Blackhead, when you are investigating a death. My first rule as a detective is this: rule nothing out, and rule everything in. That is zee way you find out zee truth."

"Do you think it was an animal that did all this?"

"For now, I think only that there have been a number of deaths, and I must find out what happened. It could have been an animal, yes; and it could have been a person who behaved like an animal. Now if you will excuse me, I must press on with my investigation."

He opened his satchel, carefully placed the pen and notepad inside it, and made his way across the soft earth of the allotment back towards Cemetery Road. Owen was left pondering on the detective's words. It reassured him to think that a man who was obviously a professional in the field of criminal investigation and forensic science did not exclude the possibility that an animal was behind the disappearances (and probable deaths) of Fossett, Jones, Broadbent, Formby et al. He'd actually said: "it could have been an animal, or a man who behaved like an animal."

Could it be that Lay-zyoom thought, as Owen did, that a were-cat was involved?

It was food for thought, and it gave Owen a renewed confidence in his theory.

He turned his eyes towards Stonker Edge.

Perhaps I'm looking in the wrong place, he thought. Perhaps I need to go up there and search for the were-cat on the top of Stonker Edge, if I dare.

He set off in the direction of South Stonker Lane, the improbably steep and winding road leading to the top of Stonker Edge. He got there in under half an hour and began the ascent. He was a seasoned walker but even so the road was so steep that he was breathing heavily before long.

He reached the top, turned onto Stonker Lane, and walked past the golf course. The road ahead disappeared into the distance with moorland to either side of it.

There was a wall at the side of the road and on the other side of the wall there were the fields belonging to Stonker Edge Farm. He found a gap in the wall which gave access to a path running across the fields in the direction of the farmhouse. He was about to set off walking along the path when a thick mist came rolling in off the moors. Within seconds, the farm buildings disappeared from view and he couldn't see more than a few yards ahead.

Owen began to shiver, and not just with the low temperature caused by the mist.

Images of Bigfucka losing his foot came into his mind.

What if the bloody were-cat is here now? He thought. It could be watching me, stalking me. And I won't be able to see it until it's on me.

He turned around and hurried home.

I'm going to come back, he told himself. I'm sure it's up here. I'm going to come back and make sure I find it and film it.

Chapter 16

Nigel Gresley headed for the toilets at his place of work.

He visited the toilet several times a day to get some privacy and to let his mind wander. Often when it did, he would fantasise about an alternative life, far happier than the one he had. It would be a life without his nagging wife, without his spoiled and ungrateful children, and most of all, without his mind-numbing job.

He would picture himself in his mind's eye leaving local authority employment to set up a greengrocery shop in the Huddersfield conservation area of Edgerton, or its near-neighbour Lindley.

All the fruit and vegetables sold in his shop would be imported from Provence and Languedoc and other French regions the names of which escaped him. This would guarantee success, as his English customers would be dazzled by the colours and flavours of the goods on offer. The shop would be called 'Monsieur Legume' in recognition of the French origins of the produce sold.

Sometimes, in Nigel's more extreme flights of fancy, Monsieur Legume would be more than merely a shop; he would become a real person acting out the exciting life that Nigel so desperately wanted in preference to his own miserable existence.

Monsieur Legume, who was a detective, would spend his days fulfilling the dreams of his frustrated creator, wandering around the French countryside, enjoying fine French food and wine, and solving the murder cases that were an all too common part of French rural village life.

At each village Legume would endear himself to the locals by solving a murder case that had proved insoluble to the bumbling efforts of the local Gendarmerie. He would follow a trail of cryptic clues then piece them together with an infallible logic and quickly apprehend the murderer who had been ruining life in the village for its ordinary law-abiding citizens.

Afterwards, Legume would bid an emotional farewell to the simple French villagers whose inbred tears of gratitude were ample reward for the work he had done in putting the villains behind bars.

He would contemplate life and would move on to the next village to deal with the next difficult case, for that is what he did: he philosophised, and he solved murder cases.

It often occurred to Nigel, as he ruminated on the subject of Legume, that the French knew very little about their own language.

French people would pronounce the name "Legume" with a hard g, like the g in the word groom, so that "Legume" would sound like "Lay-goom".

Nigel disagreed with the name being pronounced in that way. To him, it should always be pronounced with a soft g, more like a z, or the s in the word "casual", so that it would be spoken as "Lay-zyoom". That sounded far more sophisticated, and was, to his ear, far more French.

Today, in the toilets on the 8th floor of Kirklees Towers, Legume (Lay-zyoom) soon put in an appearance. The Great French Detective, whose reputation stretched from Provence all the way to Normandy and beyond, emerged from the recesses of Nigel's mind and went about his business, trekking over vividly imagined landscapes and solving murders. But today these were not the landscapes of southern France; they were the landscapes of Huddersfield, Nigel's hometown, to which Legume had temporarily relocated, in order to apply his talents to solving the recent spate of unsolved murders that had taken place there.

An hour later Nigel emerged from his reveries and realised that he had made no progress with his work for the day. He stood up, left the cubicle, and headed back to his desk.

Waiting for him on his desk there was a box of documents that had been compiled by wonks in Whitehall. On the top was a label which read: 'Regulations and Guidelines for the American President's Visit to Huddersfield'.

Nigel was an LGO (Local Government Officer) who worked for Kirklees Council.

His contribution to the welfare of the citizens of Huddersfield consisted of reading through the endless river of policy documents emanating from central government, digesting the contents of each, then turning them into papers of manageable size for consumption by the directors and decision makers of Kirklees Council.

Typically, a government policy document would run to two hundred pages of densely-packed text, while Nigel's version of the same document would consist of only one A4 page, double-spaced for easy reading.

Nigel had once been a member of a large department of Policy Officers within Kirklees Council, but due to the cutbacks that had been carried out by central government, he was the only one left. He'd been spared the axe for two reasons: firstly, he was the longest-serving member of the department; and secondly, he was capable of getting through more work than anyone else in the history of Policy Officers.

Even though the department had employed over thirty Policy Officers five years previously, and was now down to only one – Nigel - and the river of documents from Whitehall had not slowed one iota, indeed, if anything, had become faster-flowing than ever, Nigel was able singlehandedly to keep on top of the job. This was because he had developed a unique system which made him more efficient than anyone else.

Nigel never read the documents that were given to him to condense into A4 summaries.

He preferred instead to use two processes which he privately referred to as "assimilation" and "osmosis".

Assimilation meant reading only the top line and bottom line of each page of a policy document and relying on instinct, experience and judgement to interpolate what the document was getting at. It was an approach that had stood Nigel in good stead for his degree (a third in Communication and Cultural Studies from Oxford Polytechnic) back in the seventies.

Osmosis involved looking at each page of a document (or as many pages as he could bear to look at) without ever reading any of the text whatsoever. Nigel believed that at an unconscious level, the meaning of the policy documents would be made apparent to him via Osmosis and would emerge clearly in his A4 summaries.

He frowned and opened the box.

Then he took out the documents it contained and placed them in a neat pile to his left.

He perused them one by one, randomly switching between osmosis and assimilation, and in no time at all he'd condensed hundreds of thousands of words of vital information prepared by the wonks into a handful of A4 pages which he sent upstairs to the executive officers of the council for implementation.

Chapter 17

M. T. Dross, the Kirklees Director of Tourism, was on the committee charged with organising the V.O.Z day celebrations in Huddersfield.

The committee met for the first time in the Magic Rock, a pub that was far enough removed from the town centre to have emerged intact from the carpet-bombing a few months previously. The first motion that was carried was that they should have a pint or two of real ale purchased out of civic funds, as they were all in need of refreshment. Duly refreshed, they got down to business.

"I've got an idea," said Dross. "When the President comes, we should show him our town properly, not just the remains of the centre. We ought to show him the whole thing, because his visit will get shown on American TV, which means Huddersfield will be shown on TV with him, and that will bring tourists flocking to us from all over America if they see the parts that haven't been bombed."

"And how do you propose doing that? Just how can we show the president our entire town?"

Dross assumed the knowledgeable expression of a leader.

"I know just the way," he said. "We'll arrange a trip for him up to the top of Stonker Edge. We'll take him right to the precipice. From there he'll see the entire town spread out below him. And while he's admiring the view, the American news companies are going to be showing images of it all over America. Huddersfield will become famous and tourists will come in droves."

The committee members all nodded.

"A trip to Stonker Edge, what a great idea, M.T. Motion passed!"

M.T.'s idea was the first to go on the long list the committee came up with that day. The list was duly sent to the council's chief executive for approval. He read through it then he read through the briefing notes he'd received from Nigel Gresley about the precautions to be taken to ensure that the President's visit went smoothly. It was clear to him, given the guidelines he'd had from the wonks in central government, as condensed by Gresley, that none of the items on the list posed any threat whatsoever, and he approved it in full and sent it back to the V.O.Z. committee for implementation.

Chapter 18

A C-17 Globemaster III touched down at Heathrow. It was one of the largest transport aircraft available to the American military. As it pulled up on the tarmac a group of airmen emerged, opened the doors of the hold and went inside. They emerged a few minutes later driving the specially adapted Cadillac limousines that were to be used for the President's motorcade. There were ten in all. The men went into the hold again, and this time appeared on Harley Davidson police motorbikes that would drive ahead and at the flanks of the motorcade. They parked all the vehicles in a neat line on the landing strip next to the huge aircraft.

An hour later, the President's personal airplane - Air Force One - touched down on the same airstrip and taxied up close behind the C-17 Globemaster. Members of the American press climbed out – all of them male – followed by an army of CIA men wearing their usual uniforms of dark suits, white shirts and dark ties, dark glasses and earpieces. Then the President himself emerged and stood at the top of the steps, posing and waving his hat. For once, there was no waiting band of admirers on the ground below, just a bunch of members of the American and British media, but he made the most of it, smiling and looking upbeat.

He turned his head so that he could speak to Tyler, who was just behind him.

"Why didn't you arrange to have a crowd of admirers waiting for me Tyler? God-dammit, you've made me look like an unpopular ass-hole!"

He turned to look at the press once again, a beaming smile on his flabby face, and descended the steps. When he got to the bottom, he cast his eye approvingly over the long line of cars. "This better be the biggest motorcade any American President ever had, Tyler."

"It is, Mr. President. I made sure of that."

They climbed into the lead car and the motorcade set off for the gates in the Heathrow fence that were open to let them through. British police on British cop bikes were waiting for them outside the gates. Doughnut nudged Tyler and pointed at them.

"See that," he said. "Those Brit cop bikes aren't any-where near as cool as our American Harleys. We're winning the P.R. war already."

The motorcade proceeded through London with great fanfare to Buckingham Palace, where Doughnut was met by the queen. She was waiting for him at the doors of the palace. He climbed from his limo and headed confidently over to her, and then realised that he wasn't sure whether he should shake hands or bow, as he hadn't listened to the briefing he'd been given on Presidential protocol when meeting other heads of state.

I don't know what I'm meant to do, but I'm certainly not going to be obsequious, he told himself.

He reached the doors of the palace holding out his hand. The queen looked puzzled for a moment before taking it, and even more puzzled as he shook it vigorously.

"I'm pleased to meet you, Queen Elizabeth" he said, fumbling in his trouser pocket for his mobile with his free hand. It slipped from his grasp and he got frustrated.

"Tyler, get my mobile and take a picture, will you?" He said.

Tyler stuck his hand in the President's trouser pocket and grimaced as he probed with his fingers, a look of mild disgust crossing his face for a moment. Eventually he got hold of the mobile, pulled it out, and took a picture of the queen and President together.

Doughnut and the queen then went inside the palace and the Queen did the meaningless small talk with him at which she excelled after decades of practice, then she gave a discrete signal to one of her uniformed courtiers who politely informed Doughnut that his audience with the Queen was at an end. Doughnut stood up, and, despite himself, did a sort of half-bow and left, escorted by the courtier.

He got back in his car and the motorcade proceeded along Whitehall to Downing Street.

"I think that went very well Tyler," said Doughnut. "The Queen is real nice, unlike their Prime Minister. She talked to me about her dogs and let me pet one of them, and got one of her butlers to make me a cup of tea. They have uniforms, you know. As soon as we get back to America, I'm going to get some uniformed butlers in the White House."

The motorcade proceeded along Whitehall without difficulty as the police had made sure that no other traffic could enter the road while the President was on it. This caused untold fury all around London, as thousands of cars backed up in every direction unable to move. Eventually the procession reached Downing Street, and the gates to the street were opened to accommodate Doughnut's limo. The rest of the limos had to wait outside because there wasn't room for them.

Tyler passed his laptop to Doughnut as their car drew to a halt.

"Look at this Mr President," he said.

Doughnut scrutinised the screen. There was a news bulletin on it:

"Anonymous government sources have today confirmed that the President is having an emergency briefing from the British Prime Minister to assist him with domestic policy affairs at home."

His brow furrowed.

"Why, that treacherous limey bastard. He's done exactly what we didn't want him to do. Get onto the White House right away. Tell my P.R. men to deal with this."

He noticed something else on the screen, a news item about a tragic incident in Jacksonville. A huge explosion had destroyed several buildings near the famous Jacksonville Beach, including restaurants and shops. There had been scores of casualties.

"My God, Tyler," said Doughnut. "We have to get this over with and get back to Washington before that lunatic Havoc blows up the entire eastern seaboard."

He climbed from the limo all smiles as cameras flashed. The press were eager to talk to him, but lines of police held them back. He walked to the door of Number 10 with Tyler following a few paces behind.

"Is it true you've got problems in America that you can't handle?" One of reporters shouted.

"Why do you need our help?" Another shouted.

Doughnut gave them a bland smile and waived.

Camemblert was waiting on the steps of Number 10. Doughnut paused just before he got there and turned to face the press.

"This is just a regular state visit to cement relations between our two great countries!" He shouted. "It's nothing to get excited about!"

Then he grinned and waived again, shaking hands with the PM for the cameras. The two men jostled with each other, each one wanting the other to enter first. They both knew that the first to enter is seen as being less important than the second to enter. The PM had height on his side, but the President had weight on his side. After a savage contest lasting well over a minute, they both got stuck in the doorway for a moment, then somehow got free of it and staggered through into the entrance hall at the same time.

Tyler followed closely behind.

Johnson was waiting inside, and he swiftly closed the door behind them.

"Are you satisfied, Prime Minister?" He asked under his breath.

"What? What was that?" The PM wheezed crossly. He was red-faced and out of breath, as was the President.

"Nothing, Prime Minister."

"Right then" said the PM turning to Doughnut, who was mopping his sweating brow with a white handkerchief, "Let's go through to the drawing room, shall we? Follow me."

He led Doughnut and Tyler along the hall, past the many portraits of glorious former Prime Ministers such as Margaret Thatcher, David Cameron, and Tony Blair, which lined the walls, and through a door into an impressive lounge. Johnson followed them in.

"Take a seat," said the PM.

Doughnut collapsed into a chair, which groaned with the effort of supporting his weight. Johnson shuddered. Then Doughnut wrung out his sweaty handkerchief onto the expensive carpet, and Johnson shuddered again. Doughnut thrust the handkerchief back in his pocket and looked around the room, frowning.

"The stuff in here looks like it went out with the Ark," he said.

Johnson raised an eyebrow.

"It's got history," said the PM. "I suppose you won't appreciate that, because you don't have much of that sort of thing in America."

"History is bunk. Anyway, that's enough of the small talk. Let's discuss my problem, that is, er, my situation."

The PM smiled.

"Let's have some drinks, shall we?" He replied. "It's a bit early for gin and tonic, how about a tea or coffee?"

"I'll have a large cappuccino," Said Doughnut.

"I'll have an americano please," said Tyler.

"Johnson, did you hear that? Get the American President a large Cappuccino whatever that is, and get me my usual tea."

"Very good Prime Minister."

Johnson left the room.

Doughnut glared at Tyler.

"Don't just sit there, make yourself useful, that's what you get paid for. Go and help the man make some coffee," he said. "That way I might get it done the way I actually like it."

Tyler reddened and followed Johnson into the kitchen.

"Where's your Gaggia?" He asked.

"My what?" Said Johnson.

"Sorry, I meant: where's your coffee espresso machine."

"We don't have one," said Johnson. "We have this instead."

He opened a battered-looking cupboard and took out a catering-sized tin of Nescafe coffee powder.

"Cutbacks, you know," he explained.

Tyler stared at it in disgust.

"You mean, you don't grind your own coffee from coffee beans?"

"No," said Johnson. "We get the kindly people at the Nescafe factory to do it for us."

"Your boss the Prime Minister seems okay. Can't you persuade him to get a decent coffee machine to entertain his guests with?"

"I'm afraid I can't. The Prime Minister is a capital fellow, but at times he's a bit of an arse. What's your chap like? The President I mean?"

"Doughnut? He's pretty much a full-on ass-hole all the time."

While this conversation was taking place, the P.M. and Doughnut were continuing with their Summit Meeting in the lounge.

"Now, where were we? Oh yes, your little problem," said the PM.

"Situation," said Doughnut. "My *situation*. It's not a problem. I'm dealing with it. I've got zombies in my country and I've got an exterminator on their case. But it won't hurt me to hear how you got rid of yours."

The PM smiled again.

"Oh, you mean you yanks might be able to learn something useful from us brits, do you? That makes a change."

"Why don't you just cut the crap and get on with telling me what I crossed the Atlantic to hear?" Doughnut growled.

"With pleasure," said the PM, making his pleasure all too evident. "The zombies are pretty hard to kill, as you may have found out. I'm told you can take them out with a head shot if you have the firepower, but it takes time, as you have to track them down and deal with them carefully one-by-one, and time isn't on your side. Apart from that, the only solution seems to be high explosive, which causes collateral damage, and is bad for the ratings. If you were to simply use high explosives, you might not get elected for a second term."

"So? What's the answer?"

"Well, what I did was this: I got in touch with their leader. I told him we were willing to live side-by-side with the zombies as long as they didn't try to take over, and that we'd let them have a town they could call their own. I gave them a place that's not very important in the scheme of things. It's called Huddersfield, and I gave them an incentive to go there by laying on a supply of fresh food for them."

"Fresh food?"

"The two-legged variety. I got some dangerous prisoners released from gaol and had them bussed in to Huddersfield. The zombies loved it. Then I arranged an air-strike and wiped them all out."

"What about your own people? Didn't the bombing kill a lot of them, too?"

"I managed to get most of them evacuated, so it was mainly zombies that were killed. And anyway, it was only Huddersfield. We chose it because it's a place that doesn't matter. The other important thing you need to know is that I've thought of a way of buttering up the survivors. I'm holding a zombie clog-dancing festival in the town, or what's left of it."

Doughnut's eyes widened.

"What the hell are you talking about?" He asked.

Just then the door to the lounge opened and Johnson came in carrying a silver tray with tea, coffee, milk and sugar on it. He set it down on an occasional table in front of the PM and handed a mug each to Doughnut and Johnson, and a delicate bone china cup on a saucer to the PM, who took a sip from the cup.

"Let me explain," he said with a sigh, putting his cup on the saucer and placing it carefully back on the tray. "After we bombed Huddersfield, the residents could have been a little peeved. Some of them might have decided not to vote for me at the next election, not that I would have been bothered because most of them didn't vote for me anyway. But the point is, we couldn't blow the town up without putting in place measures to rebuild it. The trouble is, that sort of thing costs money. So, I've come up with a way of doing it on the cheap."

The P.M. paused for dramatic effect. He could see that Doughnut and Tyler were hanging on his every word, and he intended to keep them dangling to make the most of it.

"What way?" Doughnut asked after a while.

The P.M. smiled. It was a smile that was calculated to irritate, and it did. Doughnut scowled.

"I'm going to hold a festival there to commemorate our great victory in the war against the zombies. That'll attract inward investment, get money spent in the shops – well, those shops that're still standing, anyway – and generate revenue to enable the townsfolk to rebuild their town. And just to make sure that everyone gets the message, and most of them get out to vote for me at the next election, I'm staging these festivals all over the country.

Now, I know what you're thinking: what's clog-dancing and what's it got to do with zombies?"

He paused to take another sip of his tea.

"The people of Huddersfield have this special form of dancing they do, called clog-dancing. I'll spare you the details. Suffice it to say that it's quite barbaric, but it seems to keep them happy. Anyway, I wanted to tie in zombies with something local to Huddersfield, as the town had played an instrumental role in getting rid of the zombies, so I came up with a festival featuring people in fancy dress as clog-dancing zombies. Do you see?"

"I'm beginning to. Tyler, are you taking notes?"

Tyler, who had been busy drinking his coffee, quickly put it down and took a pen and notepad from his pocket.

"Yes, Mr President."

"Get this down. I want you to find me a hick town that votes Democrat and won't be missed if we blow it up."

"How about somewhere in the Appalachians?"

"Perfect, as long as it has roads on it that can take a greyhound bus full of prisoners. Plus, we need to think of a theme for a festival we can hold afterwards to make the survivors feel good about what we've done to them. A theme that'll make them feel involved, and celebrated. After all, they're the ones who'll have made all the sacrifices."

"How about getting some banjo players Mr President?"

"What?"

"You know, like in the movie 'Deliverance'. That's what they all do in these hick settlements in the Appalachians. They all play the banjo. So we could have a festival with Zombie banjo players. We could call it 'Duelling Zombie Banjos'."

"I've seen that movie, it's terrific. Yeah, you know something? We might even get a hit single out of this, or an album. 'Duelling Zombie Banjos', I like it. Get that down, Tyler."

"I'm going to show you how it all works in practice," said the PM. "We're going to visit the town of Huddersfield tomorrow and show you the celebrations taking place. But you'll know that already, from your itinerary of course."

"Of course," said Doughnut. "Excuse me, where are your facilities?"

"Down the corridor."

Doughnut stood up and motioned with his head for Tyler to go with him. Tyler followed Doughnut into the corridor. They went together into a pokey little room with only three cubicles in it, one of which had the words 'Prime Minister' on the door. Doughnut went in.

Oh, no, please God, no, thought Tyler.

He breathed a sigh of relief when Doughnut unzipped his pants without dropping them.

"What's this about an itinerary, Tyler?" Doughnut asked.

"I gave it to you, Mr President, don't you remember? It was that morning you were going out to play golf with the Speaker of the House of Representatives."

Doughnut cast his mind back to that day. He remembered Tyler giving him a piece of paper. As he'd been in a rush, he'd thrust it in his pocket without reading it.

"Oh yeah," he said. "*That* itinerary."

He turned around to face Tyler.

"Why didn't you tell me it was important?" He growled.

"I thought you knew. I-"

Doughnut pushed past him and washed his hands in a basin on the wall.

"Next time make sure you tell me," he snarled. "Now give me another one, so that I know what's going on around here."

Tyler gave the President another copy and they returned to the lounge.

"We've got a bit of a bash arranged for you in London tonight," said the PM as they entered. "What you really want to see is Huddersfield. We'll be heading up there tomorrow, but first things first. You fellows have just had a long journey and you haven't had the chance to freshen up. Would you like me to get one of my chaps to bring in your bags, so you can both take a shower and relax before we go to the first event on the itinerary?"

"That sounds good to me," said Doughnut, who was still sweaty from his wrestling match with the PM in the doorway of Number 10.

"Very good. Johnson, do the honours for the President, will you? There's a good chap."

Johnson went outside and got Tyler's bag and one of Doughnut's bags from the limo, brought them inside, and put them on the upstairs landing. When the PM heard him, he nodded approvingly.

"Just go to the top of the stairs. You'll find your bags waiting for you, and you'll easily work out where the bathrooms are."

Doughnut and Tyler looked at each other and left the room, passing Johnson as he came back in.

The PM put his hand to his ear and listened to their movements carefully. When he heard the bathroom doors close, and he was sure the President and his aide couldn't hear what he was saying, he turned to Johnson.

"They've brought over that bloody big motorcade to make us look like the poor relations Johnson," he said. "We've got to do something that'll make us look better than them. What can we do? Give me some ideas."

"How about something ceremonial Prime Minister? We're good at that."

"What do you mean?"

"We could have the horse guards out on parade, the ones with the shiny boots and helmets."

"Capital idea, Johnson. The yanks don't have anything like that, do they? We could get that other lot out too, the ones with the big furry hats."

"Bearskins, Prime Minister."

"There's no need to show off Johnson."

Chapter 19

The following morning the President's motorcade had to drive very slowly through the streets of London, flanked as it was by soldiers and officers of the Royal Horse Guards in full ceremonial dress. The President himself was called upon to inspect lines of soldiers in their ceremonial clothes in front of Buckingham Palace while the world's press looked on. He didn't have a clue what to do, but he did his best not to look foolish. The PM observed the proceedings with a satisfied smile.

"Adolf thought he'd got one over on us Johnson," he said. "He was mistaken. We're the ones who've got one over on him."

Chapter 20

Due to the many road-works on the M1, one lane of the motorway had to be cleared of all traffic to enable the President's motorcade to make the journey to Huddersfield in reasonable time. The PM also had a motorcade, although the two Rover cars it consisted of looked battered and ancient next to the presidential Cadillacs. All along the roads leading to the motorway there were miles and miles of log-jammed motorists who were unable to reach their destinations, or even move at all, because they were side-lined by the two motorcades. These motorists were all fuming. The PM smiled at them when he saw them lined up on the slip-roads.

As they passed Newport Pagnell services, Johnson held out his tablet.

"I think you should take a look at this Prime Minister," he said.

There was a news bulletin on the screen.

'Revealed: the real reason for the President's visit to England. Anonymous sources have confirmed that Prime Minister Camembert is so worried by his flagging popularity that he has invited over President Doughnut in the hope of improving his ratings. If this doesn't work, he could be gone before the next election, ousted from office by his own party, many of whom are expressing rumblings of discontent....'

"What a load of tosh," said Camemblert. "Where did that come from?"

"Don't you know, Prime Minister?"

"No I bloody well don't, otherwise I wouldn't have asked you, would I?"

"I'm pretty sure it came from someone briefed by the White House, Prime Minister."

For an instant, the PM looked puzzled; then he reddened.

"That back-stabbing yank bastard," he said.

Chapter 21

When the motorcade entered the outskirts of Huddersfield, the President looked in wonder at the tiny houses and the cobbled streets. Then, as the cars entered the town centre, he was amazed by the sight of bombed-out buildings which looked somehow familiar. He vaguely remembered seeing documentary footage of Berlin at the end of World War II. Yes, that's what this scene reminded him of.

The townsfolk had, by this time, cleared the streets of rubble, so his motorcade was able to proceed via Viaduct Street and John William Street to St George's Square.

A stage had been set up at one end of the square, and at the other end there was a marquee for the VIP's to shelter in. The ordinary townsfolk were expected to make do with the open air.

Everything was in place for the clog-dancing zombie festival.

The CIA men climbed from their cars and assembled around the president's car. The President slowly climbed out of his vehicle and took in the sight of the marquee, and behind it the once-glorious railway station which had been reduced to a heap of rubble.

The Mayor, who was wearing his tricorn hat, black velvet cloak, and ceremonial gold chain, rushed up to greet the president, closely followed by the burghers of the town, who were determined not to be left out. The CIA men immediately closed ranks to block their path.

"It's all right, let them through," said Doughnut, who knew how and when to be populist.

The two men shook hands warmly, with the burghers standing nearby, and cameramen on scaffolding at various strategic points filming the event.

"It's an honour to meet you, sir," said the mayor. "I 'ope you'll like our town and the entertainment we've laid on for yer."

"I'm sure I will. Clog-dancing zombies, isn't it?"

"That's right Mr. President, and they're very good. But first we have some 'at else to show you. Stonker Edge."

"What the hell is Stonker Edge? It sounds obscene."

"It's a geographical feature at the edge of the plateau overlooking our town. We want to take you up there so that you'll see our town properly. If you look you'll see it's on your itinerary."

"Tyler!"

"He's right, Mr. President, that's where we're going next. Then we're coming back to the centre to sit in the marquee over there with the town's movers and shakers and enjoy the zombie clog dancing festivities."

"All right, I gotcha."

Everyone got back in their cars. The Mayor climbed into his black mayoral Rolls-Royce, which was a 1950s model, and led the way. M. T. Dross was in the back of the Rolls-Royce with him.

The long line of cars proceeded along John William Street and up Westgate into Castlegate, then headed into Birkby and climbed the steep hill that led to the top of Stonker Edge.

They followed Stonker Lane past the golf club. There was nothing to be seen in any direction other than for a wall at either side of the road, and, in the far distance, the occasional cow in a field.

The mayor's car pulled up, the Presidential motorcade pulled up behind it, the P.M.'s rather smaller motorcade pulled up behind that, and the vehicles carrying the world's press and media reporters came to a halt at the rear.

M. T. Dross climbed out of the mayoral Rolls-Royce followed by the Mayor himself in all his finery.

The president's armed guards left their cars and formed a protective cordon around the President, who then left his own car, wearing his trademark red baseball cap. Police on motorcycles straddled their stationary bikes and looked around in wonder at the desolate plateau that Dross had taken them to.

The President removed his baseball cap for a moment to scratch the top of his head. A chill gust of Yorkshire wind whipped up his comb-over despite the powerful glue that had been applied by his personal hairdresser that very morning to hold it in place. He quickly jammed his baseball hat back on again.

M.T. Dross was charged with leading the group to Stonker Edge to admire the view. He looked at his O.S. map.

"This way," he said confidently, marching up the road to where he knew there would be an opening in the wall giving access to the footpath leading to Stonker Edge.

When he got there, he stopped. The wall looked as though it had once had an opening in it which had been blocked up with breeze-blocks cemented in place. Dross looked over the wall. There appeared to have once been a footpath on the other side of it, but the path had barbed-wire fences at intervals along its length which would prevent anyone from using it. Dross checked his map and turned it upside down. Then he turned it the right way up again.

"What are you doing, for God's sake?" The Mayor asked. "We've got the President of America and the Prime Minister with us. We're meant to be showcasing our town to the world. Nothing better be going wrong, Dross."

Dross felt beads of perspiration forming on his forehead and on his body beneath his clothes. He couldn't make sense of the map. He couldn't relate what was on the map to what he saw in front of him. He raised his head and looked further along the road. About fifty yards ahead he saw an opening in the wall. There was a man in a red walking jacket standing next to the opening.

"We go this way," Dross said with a confidence he didn't feel. "The footpath to the edge is just up there."

He set off walking, with a long line of people trailing behind him. He quickened his pace and left the mayor behind. He reached the opening in the wall and saw that there was a neat footpath leading from it across the field on the other side, just as he'd hoped. It was in a different place to the path marked on the map, but it seemed to lead in the right direction, towards Stonker Edge.

The man next to the opening was wearing the sort of outfit that walkers wear. That was a good omen. Dross turned to the man, who happened to be Owen Blackhead.

"Do you know if this is the path to Stonker Edge?" He asked.

"It must be," Owen replied. "It's heading in the right direction and there aren't any other paths going that way."

Dross breathed a sigh of relief.

A few cameramen and sound men ran up to join him at the head of the line of people, as did several of the CIA men.

What can possibly go wrong? Dross asked himself. It's only a field and we're only a short distance from the Edge and I've just been told by a walker that it's the right path.

Nevertheless, he felt a stirring of disquiet in the pit of his stomach.

"This way," he said cheerfully, in the most upbeat tone he could muster.

He'd gone twenty yards or so along the path when he noticed that the grass in the field was unusually long and full of thistles. He glanced around. All the fields on Stonker Edge Farm were full of long grass and weeds. That seemed somehow wrong to him. He felt another stirring of disquiet.

"Is something the matter, Dross?" It was the Mayor.

Dross felt more beads of perspiration forming on his forehead despite the chill wind that was blowing. He wiped it with the back of his hand.

"No, no. Everything's just hunky-dory," he replied.

The line of politicians and dignitaries formed a line, and followed Dross and the Mayor along the path, the cameramen and sound crews forming little groups around the line, mainly in the vicinity of the PM and the President. The CIA men fanned out. The police remained astride their bikes on Stonker Lane.

Soon, the entire crocodile of men and women and equipment was in the field, either on the path, or to either side of it, with Dross and the mayor leading the way.

It occurred to Dross that there were no cows in the fields around Stonker Edge Farm. He wondered why. He'd noticed cows in the fields belonging to the neighbouring farms. He could see them in the distance. He'd even heard a mooing sound from far away. But there were no cows nearby.

The knot in his stomach tightened. His instincts were telling him that the lack of cows betokened something sinister. He told himself it was nothing to worry about, and that the farmer must have got rid of his cows for some reason, or that he must be keeping them in a shed somewhere. He forged ahead, face set. Then he saw something in the grass, something white, like a cage. He paused.

"Dross, what is it?" The Mayor asked.

Dross realised that what he'd seen was a cow's ribcage. What could it mean?

"Nothing," he said with false confidence. "This way."

He started walking again, becoming aware now of faint movements in the grass, as if small animals were scuttling around in it.

Must be the wind, he thought, until he noticed that some of the movements seemed to be in the opposite direction to the wind. Then he thought: it could be badgers, if they have badgers around here.

Then he and the mayor heard a howl of pain.

Chapter 22

Everybody turned their heads to see a CIA man at the edge of their column fall into the long grass and disappear from view. Two of his colleagues ran over to help him.

"Aaargh!"

"Aaaaargh!"

Then they were gone, too, unaccountably, as if the grass had somehow swallowed them up. The rest of the CIA team drew their guns and surrounded the President, forming a circle around him, all of them facing away from him, pointing their weapons into the grass.

"We're going to escort you out of here, Mr President," one of them said, "head back towards that hole in the wall we came in by."

The motorcycle cops who'd been waiting by the cars heard the screams and saw the CIA men going down. They revved up their bikes and headed through the opening in the wall then set off like the cavalry in the grass at either side of the path.

Owen looked on, his heart beating rapidly. He was sure that this was a were-cat attack and that he was going to record it on video, and prove to the world, and, most importantly to his wife, that he wasn't going mad.

As he looked on, one of the motorcyclists in the grass went down, seemingly acquiring some sort of furry coat just before he did. Owen took out his mobile phone. His hands were trembling with excitement. Or was it fear? Whatever it was, the mobile dropped from his grip. By the time he'd picked it up, three more of the motorcycle cops had gone down. He raised the mobile to begin filming and then he saw a movement in the grass a few yards away. He dropped the mobile and ran for it as fast as he could, past the long line of limousines parked by the side of the road, past the golf club, and even though he had dodgy knees, and even though running hadn't been his thing for many years, he somehow kept going until he'd reached the comforting streets of Birkby far below Stonker Edge.

Behind him, events were taking an unplanned turn.

Doughnut turned around and walked back the way he'd come. His praetorian guard of CIA men barged the cameramen and sound crews who were filming them to one side in order to get through. A news reporter ran forward to get the President's comments on the situation and was pushed aside to enable the President and his men to make quick progress.

At the head of the line, the Mayor turned to Dross. On the periphery of his vision he noticed a motorbike cop falling sideways into some thistles.

"You better not 'ave fucked things up for the town of 'Uddersfield, young man," he said.

Dross felt his heart beating rapidly, and it wasn't just because of the Mayor's words. His instincts were telling him that he was facing the biggest threat of his life, but he had no idea what that threat might be. He spread out his arms.

"I haven't," he said. "I swear to God that I haven't fucked things up. This has got nothing to do with me, whatever it is."

The Mayor wagged a plump forefinger in Dross' face.

"No lad, it 'asn't got owt to do with you," he said. "But you're the one who thought of it and led us all up 'ere. And I 'ave this funny feeling that we're all going to be fucked because of you."

The Mayor looked around and noticed the same thing that Dross had noticed a couple of minutes earlier: that the grass seemed to be moving here and there, as if small animals were concealing themselves in it, and – the thought made him shudder – stalking them.

"I'm getting out of 'ere," he said.

He turned and began walking back the way he'd come.

Camemblert, who had been a few yards behind the mayor and Dross, looked at his aide.

"What the devil's going on, Johnson?" he asked.

"I don't know Prime Minister," said Johnson, "But common sense would suggest that we ought to leave, quickly."

They turned around, noting as they did so that the entire column of people that had been following them was doing the same, and in the process were colliding into each other. Some were falling over, mainly cameramen and sound men, who were disadvantaged by having things to carry, and being brutally pushed to one side by the CIA.

The CIA team soon got to what had formerly been the rear of the column, and was now the front, largely because

274

two of them had gone to either side of the President and done their best to propel him along the path at speed. They were now only fifty yards or so from the exit back to Stonker Lane, and, following in their wake, there was a long line of people, including eight very pissed-off TV crews.

The CIA men abruptly came to a halt and everyone behind them collided into each other.

The people at the back couldn't see what had caused the CIA team halt.

"Why has everybody stopped?" Camemblert asked.

"Heaven alone knows, Prime Minister," said Johnson. "Our American cousins have always been a flighty and unpredictable lot, as you know."

Two gunshots rang out across the field.

"What the devil was that?" Camemblert asked.

"I believe it was gunfire, Prime Minister," said Johnson.

Chapter 23

At the head of the line there was a dead CIA man lying next to the path. Two cats were on top of him. They'd been ripping chunks from his face until two of his colleagues had shot them.

The cats had both been hit in the torso, but apart from having holes that ran clean through them, they appeared unhurt. What's more, they looked very pissed off.

One of the CIA men turned to the other. "Oh my God," he said.

The cats crouched low, wriggling their backsides.

"They're about to pounce," said his colleague. "Quick, take a head shot."

They aimed and shot. The heads of both cats exploded. The headless torsos collapsed to the ground, legs twitching.

"What the hell were they?" Doughnut asked.

"I don't know sir," said one of the two CIA men at his side. "But don't worry. We've just got rid of the problem."

As the words left his mouth, the grass ahead of them parted in various places and heads began to stick out of it. Cat heads. Two cats appeared on the path in front of them: Henderson and Goliath.

"Oh my God," Said the CIA man again. He directed his gaze at Henderson, running his eye over his curiously flattened and spiked midriff. "What in the name of God is that?"

"Quick," said a voice behind him, "take the president back the other way."

The two men who were either side of the president turned and wheeled him around with them. They marched back the way they'd come, with a protective cordon of CIA operatives surrounding them. Just as they'd done before, they barged TV crews out of their way as they headed down the path to safety.

Meanwhile, at the head of the queue, the two men who'd been leading the way to the gap in the wall had been left behind as a rear-guard. Each had twenty or thirty zomcats attached to various parts of his body by their teeth and claws.

They both cried out the famous last words that have been spoken countless times before during the grim history of our species:

"Aaaaaargh!"

The last of the motorbike cops drove past them as they went down, retreating towards the gap in the wall as fast as his bike could carry him. Before he got within twenty yards of it, something came bounding across the field towards him. It had blades where it should have had hind legs, and the way it moved was suggestive of a giant flea, or the marvel-comic book character known as the 'Hulk'. It hit the biker with the force of a cannonball and sent him flying out of sight into a huge clump of thistles. He was never seen again.

Chapter 24

The CIA men moved as quickly as they could, given the age and weight of their commander-in-chief. It was quick enough to spread confusion amongst those ahead of them, who found themselves having to change direction for a second time to get away from the threat they faced.

The PM was forced to stop because the people ahead of him were suddenly coming towards him. The mayor, who was to his rear, barged into his back.

"I'm very sorry Prime Minister," he said, doffing his tricorn hat apologetically.

The P.M. ignored him. "What the devil can be happening now, Johnson?" He asked crossly, as panic-stricken news broadcasters and media men streamed past him, some of them jostling him in their eagerness to get away from some hidden danger he hadn't yet seen.

"I haven't the foggiest, Prime Minister," Johnson replied.

"Well, I think this is bloody shameful," said the PM, as the CIA men flanking Doughnut barged him out of the way. "They ought to show some backbone. Stiff upper lip and all that."

There was now no-one left in front of Johnson and the PM. This gave them a clear view of the path ahead all the way to the opening in the wall that they had originally entered by, but neither of them was looking at the opening. They both had their eyes fixed on what looked like a mountain of domestic cats devouring something.

Could it be, could it possibly be? Thought the PM. He looked more closely. Yes, yes it is. It's two of the CIA men. Those bloody cats are eating the CIA men.

One of the cats raised its head. It was a big ginger brute of a cat, with a midsection that looked like a circular saw. Its evil eyes seemed to glow a bright red colour.

"Johnson," he said. "Do you see what I see?"

"Yes, Prime Minister. I think so."

"What do you think we should do?"

"I think we should bloody well run."

"So do I."

Both men turned and ran back along the path, quickly catching up with the mayor, who was somewhat corpulent, and then overtaking the President and his men. The PM made a point of barging into the CIA men as he overtook them.

To either side of the path there were expensive cameras and sound booms that had been abandoned by the TV crews who had decided that survival was more important than preserving the equipment of their employers. The TV crews were running as fast as they could away from the zomcats, as was everyone else. The path couldn't accommodate everyone, so many of them were forced to run in the long grass at either side of the path.

"Aaaargh!"

The PM, who was tiring, turned his head to see a sound man go down with one cat on his head, three hanging

279

from his back, and countless others attached to his legs. The PM found extra reserves of energy and began to run faster.

"Aaaargh!"

Another sound man went down.

The once-orderly line of people was now a panic-stricken rabble charging towards Stonker Edge Farm. Not many of them were on the path any more. They had formed an amorphous mass on the path and to either side of it, and with every second that passed, another cry went up, as someone on the fringes of the rabble was brought down by the zomcats:

"Aaaaargh!"

A cameraman disappeared into the grass.

"Aaaaargh!"

The mayor's chauffeur fell, never to be seen again.

"Aaaaargh!"

The mayor went down, his tricorn hat spinning from his head.

The rabble had become a fleeing herd of wild animals being attacked by ruthless predators. The PM, who, despite the timber around his middle, jogged most days, and was therefore quite fit, was near the front of the herd. Johnson, who also kept reasonably fit, was at his side. Just behind them were the fittest of the media men; and to their rear was the president and the CIA. At the very back were the Fleet-Street reporters who spent their lives listening to gossip in pubs, getting drunk, and smoking. All these groups had others to either side of them who were being picked off by the zomcats.

It wasn't long before the amorphous mass of people had been reduced to a line once again, because all of the people on the flanks had been taken down, mauled, and eaten by zomcats. The survivors redoubled their efforts to run faster.

"Aaaaaargh!"

From the corner of his eye, the president saw that one of his CIA bodyguards had somehow turned into a strange kind of Yeti; he'd become larger, and covered in fur, and he'd unaccountably slowed to walking pace. He fell on his back, the fur that covered him seeming to writhe in glee.

The PM could see that there were cats – zomcats he now realised – heading their way from the grass at the side of them. But he could also see an escape route. Directly ahead there was a large patch of bare earth. On the other side of the bare earth there were zomcats which, by rights, should have been crossing it to attack them. Instead, they were carefully walking through the grass at the edges of the bare earth, taking the long way around in order to get into position to attack.

It was as if they were somehow frightened of crossing the patch of bare earth.

The PM realised that if only he could reach the bare earth before the zomcats got to him, he'd be safe.

He suddenly became aware of a vile smell. It was like the smell of silage, or manure, but rather worse. Still, this was hardly the time to worry about bad smells.

He accelerated, as did Johnson. They were side-by-side, arms pumping and chests heaving.

He was only five yards away from the safe patch of bare earth.

Four yards.

Three yards.

Two yards.

One big stride.

He'd made it.

Then a curious and most unexpected thing happened.

The ground seemed to open up and swallow him.

Too late, he realised that he was up to his neck in shit.

Behind them, a TV crew saw what had happened and tried to stop, but the people behind them rushed forward and pushed them in. The President, when he got there, could see that there was a pool of shit right in front of him, but as the last of his CIA protectors went down covered in zomcats, he felt he had no choice. He took the plunge, with Tyler at his side, and began to flail around desperately.

"Help!" He called out at the top of his voice. "I'm drowning in shit!"

This was typical of the reaction of most of those who made it to the cesspool.

The P.M. wasn't at all worried about it though. Like most British Prime Ministers, he seemed to have an instinctive knack for swimming in shit. It was as if he'd born to swim in it. He doggy-paddled around in it quite happily, barking orders to his aide.

"Johnson, take out your mobile and call Whitehall. Get them to send a fleet of Chinook helicopters over here right away equipped with rescue winches. Tell them to get the army up here while they're at it."

Of the two hundred plus people who'd ventured up to Stonker Edge, only twenty-four survived to jump into the cess-pit. The rest were taken down by the zomcats before they got anywhere near it.

The twenty-four survivors now paddled around calling for help. The cess-pit was circular, with zomcats perched all around the perimeter of it, watching the proceedings. Occasionally someone would think to paddle near to the edge, hoping to cling to the shore for support, but would soon change his mind when confronted by a snarling zom-cat.

After what seemed like a very long wait, the Chinook helicopters arrived. They'd been summoned from RAF Oldham, and were manned by teams of rescue specialists. They winched the survivors on board and took them to the Huddersfield Royal Infirmary.

Unfortunately, due to the PM's policies, the Accident and Casualty department had been closed at the Huddersfield Royal infirmary, and after an annoying delay while the P.M. remonstrated with the medics for their refusal to treat him on the grounds that they lacked the facilities, the Chinooks had to take off again and land in the car park of the Calderdale Royal Hospital in Halifax, which had the only accident department for miles around.

An airman ran into the hospital and organised a porter with a hosepipe to hose down the casualties with jets of cold water. Due to the fact that they were caked in smelly stuff from head to toe, which had got right into their clothing, the medics insisted that they all had to strip off their clothes for the hosing session, before being allowed to enter the hospital. Once in casualty, they were sent to triage, where it was determined that none of them was a priority for treatment. Doughnut discovered to his dismay that this meant that he had to wait for over six hours before an NHS doctor would see him.

"God-damned limey medics," he snarled. "What kind of a cockamamie set-up is this? I would've got treated more quickly if I'd flown back to the states and got admitted to a hospital there."

He, the PM and the rest were given white hospital gowns to wear while waiting for their treatment. They were told to sit in the waiting room with the rest of the patients. These included a group of drunken Halifax Town football supporters who were proudly sporting various injuries from a fight they'd been in; a man who'd self-medicated with LSD, and was intermittently charging around the room on all fours, while snarling like a dog, and a young man who'd got his penis stuck in a bottle. Doughnut heard the young man offering up an explanation for his condition to the doctor. He could tell by the look on his face that the doctor found it as implausible as he did.

"What kind of an operation are you running here, Tarquin?" Doughnut asked.

"What do you mean?"

"I mean it's far too slow and the place is full of goddamned lunatics."

A football supporter overheard Doughnut and glared at him.

"Are you fuckin' startin' pal?" He asked.

Doughnut shook his head and turned away.

"Hey, ball-brain, I asked you a fucking question. Don't you fucking ignore me. Are you fucking startin', pal?"

"Gentlemen," said Johnson in his patrician tones. "There is no need for any unpleasantness. The American President was simply being - er - rather American."

The football supporter stood up, and this time he glared at Johnson.

"Are you a puff?" He demanded.

"I don't think so," said Johnson. "But what exactly is a puff? Do kindly tell me, and I'll let you know."

"Oh," said the football supporter. "Fucking clever bastard, are we? Fucking clever bastard, eh? Well, we'll see how clever you are when I get me fucking hands on yer."

He raised his fists and started hopping towards Johnson, a mode of locomotion necessitated by the fact that he'd broken his ankle in the fracas he'd been in. As he was drunk, he soon fell over and concussed himself on a low table covered in old magazines that had been provided as entertainment for the patients. He opened his eyes briefly and looked at the table.

"That table shouldn't 'ave been there," he said. "Ah'm gonna sue this place for every penny it's got."

Then he passed out.

"It's probably best to speak soto voce," Johnson said to Doughnut.

"What the hell do you mean?" Doughnut asked.

Tyler leaned close to Doughnut and whispered in his ear.

"He means you should speak quietly so as to avoid trouble, Mr President. Just remember we don't have the CIA with us and it's like downtown Baghdad in here."

"You mean we're in a war zone?"

"We might as well be, Mr President."

Doughnut turned to the P.M. again.

"What were those things that attacked us Tarquin? Were they pumas or something? Because I didn't know you had things like that in England."

The PM wasn't sure how to respond. He didn't want to admit that they were zombie-related.

"They were," said the PM. "They were – er - let me see." He turned to his aide. "What do you think they were, Johnson?"

There was a long and embarrassing silence as Johnson racked his brains.

"They were beasts, Mr President," he said at last.

"Beasts?"

"You've heard of the Beast of Bodmin Moor?"

"No, what the hell's that?"

"It's a modern English legend Mr President," said Tyler. "There's this place in England called Bodmin Moor. The legend has it that there's a beast that lives there which resembles a large cat. It's known as the Beast of Bodmin Moor."

"Precisely," said Johnson. "And today we discovered that there are beasts on Stonker Moor as well. We were attacked by the Beasts of Stonker moor."

"Adolf Doughnut!" A nurse's voice rang out.

Doughnut stood up and went for his treatment, followed by Tyler.

The P.M. leaned close to Johnson.

"Genius, Johnson," he said. "That's how we'll sell it to the public. We'll tell them there are beasts on Stonker Moor. That way we don't have to admit that there are zomcats on the loose. If we did, Johnny Public might flap a bit. But if we tell him there are beasts on the moor, he'll keep calm and just stay away from the moor."

At that moment the man who had self-medicated came charging past.

"Apart from one or two lunatics of course," he added.

Eventually, the casualties of the cess-pit were all treated for their immersion in ordure, and were able to leave the Calderdale Royal Hospital.

Doughnut, Camemblert and the other survivors of the ill-fated trip to Stonker Edge missed the Huddersfield zombie clog-dancing festival which had to go ahead without them, and was a great success, apart from the absence of the expected VIP's, and apart from the fact that five more Huddersfield residents vanished without trace during the festivities.

Doughnut, Camemblert, and their aides were helicoptered to Heathrow, where Doughnut and Tyler said farewell to Camemblert and Johnson. The American contingent then took off in Air Force One, heading for Washington DC.

Camemblert turned to Johnson as Air Force One ascended towards the grey blanket of cloud high above their heads.

"I think that all went rather spiffingly well in the end, don't you Johnson?" He said.

"Spiffingly, Prime Minister," said Johnson. "Absolutely spiffingly."

The End

THANK YOU

To my readers:

Thank you for taking the trouble to read my novel. If you enjoyed it, please talk about it, and please urge your friends to buy a copy. Oh yes, before I forget, please give it a favourable review on Amazon, Facebook and Twitter if you have the time.

   Your help is very much appreciated.
   Many thanks.
   Jack D McLean

Also by Jack D McLean

Celebrity Chef Zombie Apocalypse
Thatchenstein
Confessions of an English Psychopath
Keeping Me

All published by Next Chapter

Manchester Vice
Written under the pen-name Jack Strange
Published by Coffin Hop Press

About the Author

The mysterious Jack D McLean hails from the town of Huddersfield, in West Yorkshire, England. He's a man with a checkered past, having worked in a morgue, been a labourer, and a salesman. He's dug holes... professionally (to what end, he refuses to say – sales? corpses? possibly both?), even more terrifying – he's a former Lawyer.

He enjoys parties and keeps himself fit (the kind of fit that makes you think he may engage in fisticuffs with Vinnie Jones on a semi-regular basis, or possibly drink stout with both hands while also throwing a perfect game of darts.) He is allegedly married with two adult daughters. They have yet to be located for comment.

https://www.nextchapter.pub/authors/author-jack-mclean

Praise for Jack D McLean

"Simultaneously fascinating and uncomfortable"
Christine Morgan's world of words

"his style is one of the most unique I've ever seen"
Briar's Reviews

"stomach churning."
Law Society Gazette

"shocking, and at times twistedly hilarious…"
Fred Casden's Basement

"razor sharp wit, as well as bloody, gory and insanely funny…"
Char's horror corner

Lightning Source UK Ltd.
Milton Keynes UK
UKHW012133120421
381888UK00001B/147

9 781034 741794